Pearl

Debra Funderburk

Burkwood Media Group

P O Box 28449

Charlotte, NC 28229

Burkwoodmedia.com

Ordering Information:

Quantity Sales. Special discounts are available on quantity purchases by associations, book clubs, and others. For details, contact the publisher at the address above. Orders by U.S. trade bookstores and wholesalers.

Printed in the United States of America

ISBN: 978-0-692-18414-1

Acknowledgements

Special thanks to The Charlotte Write to Publish group who has taught me how to be a better writer. I am appreciative for the ongoing support.

To the friends and family who encouraged me on this journey.

Lastly and certainly not least, Ron, my supportive husband who believed in this story before it was a story.

Dedication

To the late E.W.

My inspiration for Pearl

Prelude

Pearl's secret was out. Her life as she had come to know it was over. It didn't matter about the last fifty years spent building a life in Anna and earning the respect of the townspeople; it was now destroyed.

It also didn't matter that she was the matriarch, a woman of prestige, quick to help and organize events, eager to pursue a cause or the one who orchestrated black tie affairs and charity events. None of those things mattered now as Pearl lay in a cold dark hospital room, voiceless and alone. The intense smell of disinfecting pine and antiseptic was enough to make the dead rise, but she was unable. Helpless, her only view was the dingy tile on the ceiling. How had she arrived at this place? What would become of her now?

 The sound of machines seemed rhythmic to the rise and fall of her breath. It confounded her, but there was nothing she could do. There was nothing and there was no one.

The staff was kind enough to her, each day a middle-aged woman would come in to check her vitals, give her a sponge bath while humming a familiar tune, but that was her only visit. Pearl could occasionally hear whispers outside her room of the secret and by now knew it was spread through town.

Time went by aimlessly blending the days and nights together, and it seemed a lifetime. Suddenly her thoughts were interrupted. A young woman entered her room. Dressed in scrubs and a white coat, hair pulled up in an unkempt ponytail and thick framed glasses, she smiled at Pearl.

"Well, Mrs. Swanson, I see you have decided to join us. My name is Dr. Parker, and I will be your doctor while you are here." She grabbed Pearl's hand as she stood at her bedside to reassure her.

"You are at Heritage Community hospital, Mrs. Swanson, you were brought here two days ago. You suffered a stroke that has left you partially paralyzed. Now I want you to squeeze my hand if you understand."

Pearl made a sound and Dr. Parker wasn't sure if it was from her trying to follow her instructions or her attempting to speak. It seemed like forever, but Pearl gathered strength to squeeze her hand.

"Good. Right now, you are unable to speak, but we believe that is a temporary side effect of the stroke. We are going to work with you to get your speech back, Okay?"

Again, Pearl squeezed her hand.

"We will start therapy right away to see if we can't get you moving. It's going to be a long road ahead, but you can do it, Mrs. Swanson, I have faith in you. Now, I will be by here to check on you tomorrow, okay? In the meantime, the nurses here will take good care of you." The doctor released Pearl's hand and gave it a gentle pat; she then wrote in her chart after which she checked her reflexes and vitals. Then Dr. Parker quietly left the room.

She was alone again.

Pearl heard what the Dr. said but could she believe it? With the looming questions of her being able to speak and move again in the back of her mind, she was afraid for her life. Who would take care of her? Would her children be there? Would she be able to return home? Being at this particular hospital was already an indicator that her life had started to change. But to what extent?

There she lay. The woman, who impacted so many lives, was now abandoned by her family and the town she spent years serving. What was going to happen to her now? There were so many questions, but no one to answer them. All she could do was wait and see.

Pearl closed her eyes as a tear rolled slowly down the side of her face. She wouldn't give in to this feeling she told herself. She would not live with regret or wallow in self-pity. She did what needed to be done in order to survive and for that she would not apologize.

At that moment, the door opened again, this time, she wasn't sure what was about to happen.

Chapter 1

Old Friends

A week earlier Pearl was sitting at her kitchen table having tea with Irene Pritchard. The women had been friends for most of their lives. Irene was the first to welcome Pearl to Anna a half century earlier.

As the women sat having breakfast, they planned their strategy for the day of packing for Pearl's upcoming move. It had been a painful decision, but she'd made it. To give up her home where she lived with her husband, raised her children, thrown countless parties, was now too much to maintain and they were prepping for the movers.

"Pearl how are you feeling now that it's almost here?" Irene inquired of her friend.

"Bittersweet." Choking back tears, Pearl takes a sip of her tea.

"Well, the good news is you will still be close by. I'm glad you decided not to move with Katelyn or Andrew, they live so far." Irene touched Pearl's hand as she spoke.

"They have their lives and families, and I don't want to interfere with that. Besides, Anna has been my home most of my life. Not without its issues though, but I like it here and I still like my independence."

The women laughed.

"The packing is not going to start by itself," said Pearl as she stood to take her dishes to the sink. Irene stuffed the last piece of muffin in her mouth, and they proceeded upstairs.

When the women reached the top of the stairs they stood for a moment looking over the landing, each in their own way appearing to reminisce over the past. Spanning the quintessential beauty of the first floor it clearly was the perfect reflection of its owner. Pearl was very classy and graceful. Well loved and respected by everyone, when she extended an invitation to any gathering very few refused to attend. A natural at entertaining and bringing people together, Pearl had won the hearts of many. Because of that she'd been the town's social secretary and event planner for years.

"We have made great memories here," Irene, breaking the silence, slipped her arm around her friend.

Pearl, biting her lip to stop the trembling, simply squeezed Irene's arm and patted her hand. All she could manage was a nod. The moment soon passed and the ladies were off to their dreaded tasks. Walking down the elongated hallway, Irene wondered if they would ever stop and just pick a room to get started. Irene had a memory for time spent in each room. Finally, Pearl assigned her a room at the end of the hall. Knowing the movers would be there in less than two weeks, Pearl wanted to pack as much as possible. The room intrigued Irene. It wasn't one she'd frequented often and was glad to be starting there. It gave her the chance to be nosey. She was good at it. Irene was just as impressed with the room like the day she saw it. Exquisite pieces were strategically placed around the room and the smell of lavender lingered in the air. Irene moved toward the double French doors facing the French provincial bed and opened them. She closed her eyes to listen to the echoing chirps of birds outside, to smell freshly cut grass and feel the bright sun resting on her face. Irene was really going to miss coming here. Pearl and she had great times in this house. There were so many memories, but memories were starting to keep her from her assigned task. Snapping back to reality, Irene closed the doors and began packing. She loved the style and taste of her friend. No one could arrange furniture nor decorate like Pearl Swanson. Truly gifted and envied by most. Irene smiled at the thought of remembering what people said to her over the years regarding Pearl. Irene wanted to do a good job, so she thought she'd better be present with what she was doing. Besides, these items were not cheap; she had to be careful with each piece. Irene took great care in wrapping the delicate pieces. Filling box after box of trinkets, it was time for her to move to the closet. Sliding boxes to line them along the wall, Irene stepped inside. *Not much in here,* thinking to herself. Scanning the closet, she saw a pile of blankets, some books, old clothing, and a few shoes. This is going to be a piece of cake and for a brief minute, she thought of a piece of five-layer chocolate cake. She'd put on a few pounds lately, turning to look at her backside. Maybe she shouldn't think about cake.

Reaching to grab the pile of blankets from the top of the shelf, an old worn metal box fell from between its layers.

"What's this?" She asked herself in a whisper.

The beat-up looking box was nothing Pearl would ever have in her house. This must have been something that belonged to Doc Swanson she thought. Even if it was, she didn't understand why Pearl would have held on to it. Maybe she wasn't aware of it.

One thing Irene Pritchard was known for was her inquisitive spirit. Her years as a journalist had been perfect for her. If there was ever something to be found out, she was the one to find it. For a split second, Irene considered not invading her friend's privacy, but she just had to know. What if Doc Swanson had secrets Pearl didn't know about? He was a great man as far as everyone knew, but what if he had hidden something from Pearl. Irene had to protect her friend, so she convinced herself she was doing it for Pearl.

She attempted to pry open the box. It was locked. Not one to be bested, Irene stepped out of the closet to look for something to pick the lock. Rummaging through a nightstand drawer she found a file. Before returning to the closet she cracked the bedroom door open and listened for signs of Pearl. After a few seconds passed, Irene called out to her.

"Pearl!.........just want to make sure you are okay!" Irene yelled.

"I'm fine. Do you need something?" Pearl yelled back.

"Oh no, just checking on you."

Irene wanted to make sure Pearl would not walk in on her prying. She returned to the closet like a thief about to steal the crown jewels and picked the lock. Her heart racing with anticipation, she heard a click and slowly opened the box. When a batch of old letters fell to the floor, Irene thought she'd hit the jackpot. Grabbing the letters, she saw they were addressed to Savannah Jones. *"Savannah Jones,"* she whispered. *Who is that?* Irene's mind was working overtime trying to remember if Pearl had ever mentioned the name. Unable to recall it, she didn't want to get caught snooping, so Irene stuffed a few letters in her pocket, put the rest back in the box and placed it between the blankets. She didn't seal the box, just pushed it to the back of the closet; she would do that another day when she returned the letters. In the meantime, Irene needed to know who Savannah Jones was, and why Pearl never mentioned her. Or did Pearl know? Maybe this really was connected to the late Doc Swanson. "Yes, I must protect my friend," she told herself.

Irene finished packing the items in the room and moved on to the next one. Mindlessly putting books in boxes and wrapping pictures, she kept thinking about the letters in her pocket. Was she making something out of nothing or was she crossing the line invading Pearl's privacy? If it was something Pearl had wanted her to know, she would have told her. But did Pearl know? And if Pearl knew why hadn't she told Irene? They had shared everything with each other. Or so Irene thought.

As the day wore on, Irene and Pearl made small talk in passing, each focusing on their own task. After a while of steady work, Pearl found Irene and interrupted her conniving thoughts.

"Let's go down and have some lunch," Pearl said. Not one to ever turn down food, Irene was eager to go.

"What are we eating?" Irene asked sealing the box she had been working on. Both ladies were in great shape for their age, even though Irene had put on a few pounds of late, she carried it well. Still, they were getting on in age and the stamina to pack and move boxes for hours was becoming difficult.

"Homemade chicken salad on a bed of lettuce, strawberries with fresh cream and whatever else we can find," Pearl told Irene.

The ladies made their way down the stairs and into the kitchen. After washing their hands, Pearl grabbed the food from the fridge as Irene set the table. The antique white scalloped plates, mint colored napkins and matching scalloped handle silverware had been placed on the antique oak tea cart that sat in front of the window across from the breakfast table. Maria must have placed them there while they were upstairs. Irene didn't remember seeing them there earlier. She strategically set each plate, napkin and piece of silverware in its proper place. Pearl taught her years earlier how to set a table correctly. Irene was not nearly as refined as Pearl but learned a lot from her through the years. After everything was set, the ladies took their seats.

The two sat quietly. Neither was sure if the other was saying grace or just glad to have a moment. Both women were in their early seventies. On most days, neither felt it or looked like it, but they were no spring chickens and they were tired whether they voiced it to the other or not.

"When will the children get here?" Irene broke the silence.

"They come in on Tuesday. It's been a long time since they've been back here," Pearl answered while wiping the corners of her mouth.

"Why do you think they've stayed away so long?" Irene asked after sipping her tea.

"I don't know. The children take up a lot of their time these days and their jobs are demanding. When I was out there last summer, I had the best time with them. They have a routine they follow that works. It just seems easier for me to go see them, I think. Maybe they want to protect the children from Anna…" Before Pearl could finish her thought, Irene quickly interjected.

"What's wrong with Anna? This is a perfectly fine town. Good wholesome place for children to learn the ways of the world without being corrupted by the people of it."

"I don't want to have this conversation with you, Irene. It's their choice, and I am willing to honor it. Let's discuss something else, please." Pearl was matter of fact with her response.

"It doesn't seem fair to me that you should always go there, and they very seldom come here," Irene managed to mumble through a bite of food. "But I will leave it alone."

"I don't mind, really. It gets me away from here for a while and soon I will be closer to them." Pearl hands Irene a napkin. "I swear you have traveled the world and interviewed dignitaries, yet you are the messiest person I know."

"Leave me alone Pearl. Don't start with me today. Besides, I was known for my interviewing skills and nothing else," Irene quirked and stuck her tongue out at her. She was going to miss her friend. They had been almost inseparable since Pearl came to town. Irene lived in Anna her entire life. Leaving only for college or to travel for work when she still had a job. She'd made the choice to remain in Anna. It was all she'd cared to know. They ate and continued to stroll down memory lane, each sharing their version of certain events.

Each would laugh at the other because that's not how one remembered something, or they reminded the other how they left out an important piece of a story. The two women had decades of stories to draw from.

When they finished their lunch, both agreed they were worn out and called the packing off until the next morning.

"Leave the dishes. Maria is around here somewhere, and she will get them," Pearl said to Irene.

"I thought she must have been here when I saw the dishes on the tea cart." Irene looked around as if Maria would turn the corner.

"Yes, she came in after we were upstairs," Pearl confirmed Irene's suspicion.

"What is she going to do when you move? She's been with you over twenty years. Surely she is not going to drive that distance to work for you?" Irene was gathering her things to leave, while continuing her conversation.

"No, and I wouldn't want her to. She is going to work for the Chatham's. They haven't replaced their housekeeper yet. It has worked out perfectly for her. I will miss her though. She has been great. She was wonderful to Katelyn and Andrew. They both love her still to this day."

"I forgot the Chatham's lost their housekeeper. Diana must be going crazy at the thought of having to wash a dish," Irene mocked.

"You know she is not going to do any domestic work. She is too afraid to crack something or break something on that artificial body. I swear if that woman has one more piece of something nipped, pulled or tucked, she is going to look hideous. Diana called the agency and had them send someone over," Pearl teased. "Come on let me walk you out. Go home and get some rest. We will talk more about the residents of Anna later."

That was music to Irene's ears. She hugged Pearl at the door and promised to call later. Irene really wanted to get home to uncover the hidden treasure she'd found earlier.

Chapter 2

The Reporter

When Irene returned home, she dropped her keys in the bowl by the table, kicked off her shoes and walked to the den down the hall. She couldn't wait to sit in her favorite chair, an old tobacco colored recliner with worn leather but it was just the way she liked it. Reclining in the chair, Irene pulled out the first letter. Careful not to rip the worn paper, she checked the date of the letter. 1964. The writing was faint, but if she squinted hard enough she could read it. Without thinking her hand adjusted the lamp on the end table to get a better view.

Dear Savannah:

Hope you have found a nice place. We are fine. Your daddy's been sick, but he won't slow down. I baked a cake for the county fair and won second place. Your brother is doing well in school. He writes when he can. I know we can't see you, but we miss you a lot.

Love,

Mom

Before Irene could start the next letter, the phone rang. Startled by the sound, she placed her hand on her chest and took a deep breath.

"Hello."

Pearl was on the other end.

"Irene, what dress do you think I should wear to the dinner on Saturday; the blue and silver one or the black and gold one?"

"Wear the blue and silver one," Irene answered, half listening.

The distraction in her voice made Pearl ask if everything was okay or was she busy.

"Actually, I just turned on the shower." An obvious lie, Irene just wanted to get back to reading the letters. "May I call you back in a bit?"

"Sure." After hanging up the phone, Pearl felt Irene was distracted, but dismissed it. Even though Irene said she was about to shower, Pearl knew her friend. Irene was either on to a hot piece of gossip or was entertaining Mr. Ridley. Keeping company with old man Ridley was Irene's secret she thought, but everyone knew it, and when he was over Irene acted strange.

Pearl also wanted to talk to Irene about the upcoming dinner. She was being honored for her years of service as the town's social coordinator. Pearl had planned everything from birthday celebrations to potluck dinners and black-tie affairs for city officials. She was good at making things come together. After forty years of service, she was retiring, so the town wanted to honor her. The call to Irene was to talk about the details of the event. Irene had been selected to spearhead it being the closest person to Pearl. When she finally got Irene on the phone, it was hard getting her to engage in conversation. Pearl gave up trying and ended the call. There was too much to do than to play into one of Irene's games. They would talk about the details of the event another time.

Irene knew she was a bit abrasive with Pearl but wanted to return to her new project of snooping. She read the next letter and made a mental note to smooth it over with Pearl later.

Dear Savannah:

Your Aunt Gertie died yesterday. I know you can't come home but thought you should know. We got your picture. You look happy. A little thin, though. Are you eating? Wish I could cook you a good meal. Your cousins will miss seeing you when they come to town. I miss seeing you too. We don't know when the funeral will be yet. I will have to write and tell you all about it.

Your dad sends his love. I love you too.

Mom

Dropping the letter and envelope to her lap, Irene wondered why Savannah couldn't go home for Aunt Gertie's funeral. This was intriguing, but not as much as finding out who Savannah was. Doc Swanson's first wife's name was Madeline, so who was Savannah? Maybe Pearl really didn't know this person.

The next letter gave a few more clues. It was dated a few years later.

Dear Savannah:

Can you believe your brother is graduating this weekend from college? We are so proud of him. I cannot wait to see him walk across the stage to get his degree. He's worked hard for it.

Can you believe there will be 35 of us to see him graduate? I don't think Benedict College is ready for all of us. Good thing it is outside. I pray we don't get rain.

We are staying at Cousin Margaret's house after the ceremony instead of making the hour drive back. Your daddy complained at first but realized it was the right thing to do.

I'm not sure how long your brother will be home with us before he leaves for the Peace Corps. We are so worried for him. But this is what he wants to do.

He really wants to see you. I'm afraid he will try and find you. We keep telling him how dangerous that would be for you, and although he says he understands, I just don't know if he really does.

I will write again soon.

Love,

Mom

One thing about being the town snoop is you get to meet a lot of people. Irene grabbed the phone and dialed a number.

"I need to call in a favor," she said to the voice on the other end. "Check into a school name Benedict College. See if there was a male "Jones" that graduated around 1975. Keep this between the two of us. Get back to me as soon as you can. Usual fee? Okay, got you covered."

Hanging up the receiver, Irene's heart beat like a drum during a parade. Hurriedly, she pulled out a pad and pen jotting down important notes for later. Listening to the chimes on the clock Irene knew it was late. She didn't care. She was too wound up to sleep. There was a story here and she was going to find it and tell it. She would not rest until the mystery of Savannah Jones was solved and if there was a connection to Doc Swanson. Irene thought Doc Swanson was an honorable man. A man of character and compassion, not to mention an outstanding doctor. Now as she really thought about it, she couldn't ever recall anyone saying anything about him that was contrary. When he and Pearl married it really was a match made in heaven. He was ridiculously handsome and regal along with Pearl being flawlessly beautiful. Their presence commanded attention everywhere they went. So why was Irene doubting him now? He'd come from an honorable family; a line of doctors from what she'd remembered. Irene stood up and stretched, ran her fingers through her hair and finally took that shower she long needed. Walking to the bedroom, the chimes from the clock reminded her how late it was. She couldn't go to bed without eating something. Completely involved in her new project, caused her to miss dinner. After the shower, she made a sandwich and fell fast asleep.

Chapter 3

Disappointment

The next morning could not come soon enough for Irene. Bright and early she made her way to Pearl's front door.

"Good morning," Irene said, as she leaned in to kiss the cheek of her friend.

"What's going on with you? You look like the cat that ate the canary. What do you have?" Pearl was curious to the bag in her hand.

"I drove into town this morning and got us hot croissants with honey cinnamon butter; freshly made mind you, and two caramel mocha lattes," Irene said teasingly as she strutted in the kitchen.

Looking at her friend strut, Pearl thought maybe one of them needed to lay off the lattes.

"Why are you in such a good mood this morning? Did old man Ridley come over last night?" Standing with her hand on one hip, Pearl waited for Irene to answer.

"No, he did not. I told you there is nothing going on between me and old man Ridley." Not looking up, Irene began to unpack the bag of goodies. "Why would you ask a thing like that anyway?" seeming slightly agitated at the suggestion.

"You rushed me off the phone last night. Then you stroll in here this morning as if you were guilty of something. So, if old man Ridley wasn't over there, what hot piece of gossip have you heard? Come on, spill it." Pearl pulled out a chair and took a seat.

Irene felt a lump grow in her throat. Telling Pearl what she knew was not an option. At least not yet. Especially since the information was found in her house. Irene took a deep breath.

"I don't have any gossip and I haven't seen Ridley in over a week. He has his life and I have mine." Fiddling with the items in the bag, she ignored Pearl's teasing. "Anyway, what did you decide about the dress?"

"Somehow I don't quite believe you," Pearl gazed at Irene with a distrusting look, "but I will leave it alone for now." So, she let it go. "I decided to wear the blue and silver one."

Finishing their breakfast, the women resumed their job of packing. Irene couldn't wait to get back to her room from the day before. Eager to exchange the letters for more, she was ready to get to work.

Pearl interrupted Irene's inner scheming by telling her she had finished that room the night before and wanted her in another one. Irene's heart sank. What would she do now? She must get back to the previous room to make the exchange. Irene needed more information.

Pearl sensed something was bothering her. "Is something wrong?"

Irene shook her head and assured Pearl everything was fine. She must pull herself together; not wanting Pearl to suspect her scheming. To break the tension, Irene took Pearl on a walk down memory lane. It would shift any suspicions Pearl might have.

"Remember the night you and Doc Swanson had the Mayor and his wife over for his birthday? The wife had too much to drink and spilled red wine on your white carpet," Irene giggled a bit.

Pearl thought for a minute trying to remember the incident. Smiling at the memory, she responded with a hearty laugh. "Yes, I remember, she was so embarrassed. Her face was as red as the wine."

"I thought the Mayor was going to kill her that night. She wouldn't get help for the drinking. He kept making excuses for her, but that night I think it was his breaking point." Irene was good at remembering details.

"She went to rehab shortly after that night, if I remember correctly," Pearl said.

"Huh," Irene remarked. "When did they admit that's where she was? The story I kept getting was she was taking care of her mother down south."

"The Mayor told John she had to go, or he was leaving. I don't think she really had a choice." Pearl spoke as if betraying a confidence.

"Pearl, you never told me that," Irene gasped as if she was shocked.

"John swore me to secrecy, and I guess after a while I forgot about it. Besides," Pearl continued, "rehab was not something one talked about thirty years ago, and John being the town's doctor didn't want to break their trust."

"So, what else did the good doctor tell you?" Irene nudged Pearl.

Pearl moved away from her and replied, "Wouldn't you like to know?"

"Yes, I would." Irene was eager to hear more.

This was the one-day Pearl wasn't going to oblige her.

"This packing is not going to get done by itself." With that, Pearl walked down the long hall and disappeared into a room.

Irene packed in the new room, but the thought of those letters continued to linger in the back of her mind. She wanted to find out more on Savannah. The desire in her was so strong, like a dog salivating over raw meat. Unable to resist the urge, she had to go back to the first room. Ducking into the room while remaining cautious not to alarm Pearl she made her way in. Remembering to breathe, she leaned against the wall and wiped the sweat from her brow. Carefully moving toward the closet.

 The box she'd put at the back of the closet was all taped and labeled. Disappointed, she bowed her head. Irene couldn't reopen the box; not willing to risk Pearl catching her in the room. How would she explain it? No, she had to get back to the other room without being seen. The only thing left was for her contact to come through. Irene tipped out of the room unseen. Her heart heavy with disappointment, the only thing left to do was finish the task at hand.

Chapter 4

Old Man Ridley

Old man Ridley lived in Anna about twenty years. A widower at a fairly young age, he never remarried. Considered to be the most eligible bachelor in Anna, he certainly had his pick of the litter.

He'd dated various women off and on, but nothing serious developed, at least not for him. He was drawn to Irene Pritchard though. Ridley wasn't exactly sure why. Maybe it was her quick wit or her playing hard to get that made him want to spend time with her. Irene never wanted anything from him. She'd been wrapped up in her career and Ridley was okay with fitting in where she allowed him to.

A prideful woman, Irene always thought about her reputation. Being careful not to be seen with Old man Ridley too much, as to give the town anything to talk about was a big concern for her. Telling stories was her job and she didn't want anyone else to take the position. Besides, she told the news, she didn't want to *be* the news.

Irene was not without her secrets also. What most people didn't know, not even Pearl, was that Irene had old man Ridley accompany her on several business trips. He practiced law part-time, so it was never out of character for him to take an occasional trip out of town.

It was always done in such a way that no one ever noticed. Irene would have died if she thought for a second anyone suspected their tryst.

Having been married to her career, a real husband was out of the question. The relationship with old man Ridley worked fine for many years, and she liked things just the way they were.

Irene was even okay with the occasional dates Ridley went on just to throw off the suspicion of others. It was her suggestion.

Irene Pritchard would never admit it, but she loved old man Ridley. Only if she knew he would marry her, she'd agree in a heartbeat. Maybe not a real heartbeat, but deep down she knew she would.

Anna was the town where wayward souls traveled to in the early years. It was affluent, and an up and coming city for those looking to start a life for themselves. Everybody wanted to be a part of it. Therefore, just like everybody has secrets they don't want revealed, Anna was no different. Ridley carried his secrets too. Irene was too busy to notice or didn't care to find out, she was just enjoying their *invisible* ride.

Convinced she'd fooled the town with their relationship, her focus now was on finding the mystery of Savannah Jones. What she didn't realize was there were other secrets about to be revealed.

Chapter 5

Newsworthy

Irene left Pearl's house early that day. Being a part of the planning committee for her party, she had to get ready for the meeting. Anxiously wanting to get home to see if there were any messages was her only focus. When Irene reminded Pearl of the meeting, she was none the wiser, and they promised to talk later.

Returning home late afternoon, Irene needed to rest before going to the meeting, but also needed to know more about Savannah Jones.

She had a message that simply said, "Call me."

Irene could barely dial the number for the private investigator as her hands trembled.

"Why do you want to know about Benedict College?" The voice on the other end of the phone wanted to know.

"I came across it in something I was reading and it peaked my interest," was all Irene would say.

"What is your connection to the Jones'? Someone who worked for you?"

"No…I don't know them. Stop with the questions and tell me what you found out." Irene was short on patience, especially when she was trying to get information.

"Benedict College is a black college in South Carolina. There were four men with the last name Jones that graduated in 1975; Robert, Hubert, Wynton, and Milfred."

"Can you find out where they are from? I'm only interested in the ones that lived an hour away from the school. Remember, no one but me is to know this information. I need this ASAP." She dropped the receiver, leaned back in her easy chair and thought out loud. *"Black College? Why would Pearl have these letters? What do they mean? Did Savannah Jones work for her family?"* Irene hadn't the slightest hint to the answers, especially because Pearl didn't talk much about her family. The topic had been off limits between them and Irene never questioned Pearl's reasons, just respected her privacy. She figured Pearl would tell her one day, but never had.

As Irene leaned back in her recliner trying to rest, her mind raced with thoughts making it impossible to sleep. She had to unlock this mystery. Rising from her seat, she began pacing the floor, rocking back and forth on her heels, looking around the room as if seeking answers. Being short on time she finally dressed for her meeting. Irene knew she wouldn't be able to focus on the meeting or anything else until the full story of her current quest was uncovered.

The meeting overall went well. Everyone wanted the evening to be perfect for Pearl. She was loved and respected by all. Irene couldn't recall a time anyone had a bad word to say about her.

Irene missed most of the meeting by being lost in her thoughts. While the committee talked about guest lists and seating arrangements, she thought about Savannah Jones. The town of Anna was sparing no expense for the banquet. People near and far were making sure they had their tickets to attend. It would be the talk of the town for years to come.

When the meeting was finally over, Irene didn't linger for small talk. There wasn't any time to waste. Before she could get home, her cell phone rang. Pulling over to the nearest lot, she took the call.

"Wynton Jones lived exactly one hour away from the college. Parents now deceased were Porter and Estelle Jones. One sibling, Savannah. Whereabouts unknown."

Feeling like she'd almost hit the jackpot, Irene's heart was rapidly beating. Trying to steady her overactive nerves, she replied, "What do you mean whereabouts unknown? What happened to her? Where is the brother now?"

"Dr. Wynton Jones is a retired Chemist. He lives in Bergeron about four hours from here," explained the voice on the other end of the phone.

"It is critical that I have his contact information ASAP. Find out what happened to Savannah Jones. I don't care how much it cost, just do it!" This was the real Irene in action. The side of her that manifested in times of crisis just so she can expose someone's secret.

Her investigative skills were still intact. She could sniff out a story like a bloodhound and not let it rest until it was told.

She was respected by most as long as they were not the subject of her reporting. But others would cross the street when they saw her. Her career had been successful until her replacement came in the form of stilettos and a tight skirt. Irene often said she held no grudges, but does one really know what lies in the heart of a wounded person?

Pulling back onto the road, Irene gripped the steering wheel. A thousand thoughts ran through her mind as she aimlessly drove home.

Who are these people? Why had Pearl never mentioned them? Irene was determined to find the connection. She wasn't sure what to do with the information once she received it, but would decide that later. For now, she just needed to know.

When Irene pulled into her driveway she turned the motor of her car off. Closing her eyes, leaning her head back against the headrest, she took a deep breath. Realizing her head was starting to hurt, Irene massaged her temples. The massaging caused her to relax. Regaining her senses, she reached for the handle to open the door. Just as she opened it, there stood old man Ridley.

Looking around to make sure no one saw him, Irene asked why he was there so early. To her knowledge they were meeting later.

"It is later," he reminded her. She had fallen asleep in the car, two hours ago.

Chapter 6

Memory Lane

Pearl finally accepted the fact the town wanted to honor her years of service to the community. Although she never wanted the attention that came with her work, she appreciated it nonetheless. It made her more excited to know the event would bring her children to town. Katelyn and Andrew had their lives, but still she missed seeing them just as she knew her Mother missed her.

Sitting on the side of her bed that night holding a crystal figurine, Pearl reminisced about the children growing up and playing on the stairs. She thought about how they'd grown quickly through their high school and college years. Then the marriage of them both. It wasn't long after, the grandchildren came. Pearl wiped a tear of joy. Now a widow and empty nester, Pearl needed something or someone to cling to, but felt there was no one. Her friends were many and would be there for her, but it wasn't the same. She thought about her family, the one she'd left years earlier and without knowing when it started, she was sobbing uncontrollably. Pearl pulled herself together, rose to enter the bathroom and washed her face. Staring at the face in the mirror, she took a deep breath. *"It was the best choice for you. Look at the life you've lived,"* she said while looking at her reflection. She wiped her face again, took another deep breath and went back to finish her packing project.

Pearl knew Katelyn and Andrew would be arriving soon. There were things still needed to be done before they came. She was grateful to have time with them and the grandkids before the banquet. Her heart was full. Katelyn and Andrew promised to help her prepare for the movers. They'd also agreed to take what they wanted from the house. When their father died, they each gathered what they wanted from his personal belongings. This was different, and Pearl wanted them to have anything they desired.

After fussing over the details of her list, Pearl prepared for their arrival. She didn't want to forget one thing. From having clean sheets on the beds, to their favorite foods, this was going to be a good visit. She was determined to make it so. Pearl could hardly sleep that night thinking about seeing the children the next day. Her body on the other hand was tired and it wasn't long before she'd fallen asleep.

The next day when Katelyn and Andrew arrived in Anna, they reminded their children of how different it was. Having grown up there, they knew the unspoken rule in the town, although they never really understood it. They had no other choice but to accept it until they were old enough to leave. They made their trips back home but only when it was absolutely necessary. The two wanted their children to have a different upbringing, so they both worked hard to make that happen. They never talked much about the details of Anna to their children, only to let them know it was *different*.

This trip brought them back to a time they both wanted to forget, but for the support of their mother, they made the sacrifice. Katelyn and Andrew would however, admit Anna was a beautiful town. Immaculately landscaped, homes hidden behind mature trees and hidden driveways. But for all if its beauty and maturity lay ugly and hidden secrets. The drive through town was solemn, almost like a death.

When they finally arrived home, their mother stood in the doorway with outstretched arms to welcome them. Pearl's embrace lasted for what seemed like an eternity. It was what Katelyn and Andrew needed. Each one held onto Pearl not wanting to let her go. Pearl missed them more than she realized but would never press the issue of them returning.

After the pleasantries and awing over how the grandchildren had grown, Pearl made them all wash for dinner. She spent the day cooking Jambalaya and baking everyone's favorite treat knowing it would bring them joy. Maria came by earlier in the day to help.

Pearl was happy. Basking in the moment with her family was better than any honor she could ever receive. Sitting at the dining room table, watching each of them as they would take a bite of this, or a sip of that, made her so lost in thought, she didn't hear Katelyn ask about the movers.

"When are the movers due?" Katelyn repeated the question.

"Next week." Pearl came out of her thought to answer.

"How are you going to be ready in a week?" Looking around the house, Katelyn seemed puzzled.

"Well, what you two don't arrange to take, I will donate to local charities. There are also people I know who could use some things. It will be fine. Irene and I have packed my keepsakes each day and the movers will pack the larger things. Don't worry, it will be okay," Pearl assured them.

"Not Irene Pritchard!," said Katelyn, as if she hadn't heard anything else Pearl just said. "I never trusted that woman. It was always something about her. I never understood how one took pleasure in someone else's pain."

"She's okay. Yes, she is a busybody, and certainly has her faults, but she has been a good friend to me." Pearl felt the need to defend Irene, but knew Katelyn was correct in her theory.

"I'll leave it alone." Katelyn threw up her hands and excused herself from the dinner table.

Pearl looked at Andrew for an explanation. Taking her hand, he simply said, "She's just worried about you, we both are. And you know what this town does to her."

"Worried about me? Why? I'm fine. Why on earth would you be worried about me?"

"We both will feel better when you move closer to us, so we can keep an eye on you. He winked as he kissed her hand.

Andrew always had a way of charming his mother. From the time he learned to talk, he melted her heart. Always a good kid, she never had any trouble from him. The thought of him there now brought her comfort.

"Go spend time with your grandchildren, I'll clear the table," Andrew said matter of factly and Pearl knew there was no need to argue.

When Pearl entered the den, there was Katelyn with the children watching a comedy show.

"I wondered where you'd gone," Pearl said as she squeezed between her and Grace.

Grace was Katelyn's youngest. A very precocious thirteen-year-old, Pearl wasn't sure if she still wanted to be treated as a child or if she was a grown up today. You never knew with Grace. This night she appeared to be in child mode.

"Grandma!" she giggled as Pearl invaded her personal space. She didn't try to move though.

The three boys were stretched out on the floor. Completely uninterested in the antics of the females. Brian, thirteen and Jon, sixteen were named after their grandfather. They were Andrew's children and Keaton was Katelyn's oldest at fifteen. The children all got along well together. They were easy going, respectable and smart children.

Pearl was pleased. This is what family was supposed to feel like. She took in the moment, never wanting it to end. Andrew soon joined them, and they laughed and reminisced until the wee hours of the morning. The grandchildren had fallen asleep hours before with Grace stretched out between Pearl and Katelyn on the sofa. Not wanting to disturb them, they put blankets over them and let them sleep.

Chapter 7

The Women

Pearl and Katelyn went into town early the next morning. They left the children with Andrew, so they could have some girl time together. As the women walked down Main Street going from shop to shop, the shop owners were glad to see Katelyn and after making small talk they were off to their next store. Grabbing a quick lunch at an outside café, they decided on mani-pedi's before heading back home.

When the women arrived home, they were surprised at what they saw. Andrew had formed an assembly line with the children, and they had made tremendous progress with packing.

"What is going on in here?" Katelyn asked while dropping bags in the foyer.

"Uncle Andrew said we could go into town for a movie and ice cream," Grace was quick to respond.

"Gramma, you have a lot of stuff," Jon reminded her as if she didn't know.

"I know I do Jon. That comes from years of accumulating things. When you have lived as long as I have, you will have "stuff," too. Pearl patted his back as she passed by careful not to mess up the flow they had going.

"Are you guys ready for a break?" Andrew asked.

With a resounding yes, they reached a stopping point and headed into town for their treat.

"You sure you ladies don't want to join us," he chuckled as they headed toward the door.

"We are sure. Have fun. See you later," they both replied.

Pearl and Katelyn inspected the work that was done while they were gone. Pleased with the results, they grabbed their bags and went upstairs.

"I think I need a nap," Katelyn told her mother.

"Me too," Pearl replied, "I am tired."

The ladies went to their respective rooms. Just as Pearl was dozing off, she felt a jolt on the bed. Katelyn had climbed in beside her. "I love you Mom," she whispered.

"I love you too," Pearl smiled, and they both fell asleep.

Katelyn woke to the aroma of fresh baked bread rising from the kitchen. Gathering her thoughts, she made her way downstairs.

"How long have you been up? Where do you get all this energy from?" Katelyn smiled at her mother.

"From you and Andrew. That's where I've always gotten it from," Pearl laughed at the thought. You two were always running around here or into something that required my constant attention.

"Remember the time Daddy hired the lady to help out around here and you fired her within the first week?" Katelyn stood looking at Pearl waiting for her to recall the memory.

"I didn't fire her. I just thought we didn't need her. I didn't feel right having someone clean my house and cook in my kitchen. Special occasions were okay, but not every day. She could spend her time in somebody else's house, but not mine."

"You were always different from the other women in our neighborhood Mom. I guess that is what made you so special," she winked at her mom.

Pearl looked at Katelyn as if she was still the five-year-old with a missing tooth and pigtails waiting for Pearl to hand her a taste of something she was cooking in the kitchen.

"What is that smile about?" Katelyn cut in on her memory.

"Just a thought I had of you," Pearl confessed, "You were about five and had pigtails."

"I hated those pigtails. Mark Whitmire used to pull them every day."

"That's only because he liked you."

"He could have liked someone else for the headaches he caused me," they both laughed.

The women finished their walk down memory lane, chopped vegetables, seasoned the chicken pieces and before either one knew it, dinner was ready. They covered the food and decided to sit out on the patio until Andrew and the kids came home.

Chapter 8

The Revelation

As much as Irene loved the company of old man Ridley, she did not want to entertain him tonight.

Irene's anxiety level, beyond anything normal, would not allow her to wait to receive a call, so she made one. She'd called Ridley first and made an excuse of how she needed to work on the plans for Pearl's party. Irene knew he wouldn't question that at all. Ridley liked Pearl, so he accepted the change of plans. He didn't like last minute changes but agreed they would get together on another night. He also knew how much Irene loved Pearl and this was important to her. Again, promising him to get together soon, she abruptly ended the call in order to place the next one.

"What's the latest? asking the voice on the other end. "I need answers now. I want to know what I'm dealing with here. No…you don't ask me questions. That's my job!"

The rudeness of her tone without question made the voice on the other end know she meant business. Without any further delay, the person delivered the information.

"557-613-4878 – okay." Irene repeated the number back. "What happened to Savannah Jones? What do you mean? Nobody just disappears. Keep digging. Check death certificates, social security records, whatever else you can access. I am paying you more than enough to get this information. Just make it happen." Slamming the phone down, Irene's heart was racing. This was too good to leave alone. She would get to the bottom of this if it was the last thing she did.

Irene needed a glass of wine. Making her way to the kitchen, she reached for a bottle of Riesling and poured a glass. Sipping slowly as if each sip was the answer to this mystery she was trying to unravel. The information was replaying in her head. Talking out loud she asked questions while offering herself answers. Not liking an answer, she scratched it for an alternate one. Irene sipped, paced, and talked to herself. Right when she was about to give up and call it a night, she stopped dead in her tracks. Suddenly, dropping the glass she didn't notice the splatter of wine on her walls or floor. It didn't matter. She had just figured out who Savannah Jones is!

Chapter 9

Irene & The Mayor

The next day as the town was preparing for the event of the season, Irene received a call from Carter Henson, the Mayor.

"Irene," he said in his gruff voice when she answered the phone. "Stop by my office today. I want to talk to you about this celebration. I want to make sure we are doing everything we can to honor Pearl. Don't know what we would have done without her all these years. I will be in my office most of the day."

Irene wasn't ready to meet with the Mayor or anyone else. She just wanted time to work on the information she'd uncovered. She couldn't say no to the Mayor without having a perfect reason, and so, she agreed to meet with him.

She called Ridley to reschedule dinner but got his voice mail. It was odd for him not to take her call but figured he could have a client and busied herself getting ready to meet the Mayor.

On her drive into town, a ton of emotions visited Irene, and she wasn't quite sure how to handle them. Out of all the theories that had gone through her inquisitive head, she never would have imagined the reality of it. *"Oh, this is too good,"* she heard herself say aloud. Just wait until the good people of Anna hear this. They won't believe it.

When Irene arrived in town, engrossed in her thoughts she missed seeing the banners that lined main street with pictures of Pearl and the information for the event.

Before realizing it, Irene had pulled in front of Town Hall. She was fortunate enough to land a parking space right in front of the building. Sitting for a moment before getting out of the car to compose herself, she couldn't let anyone know just yet about her news.

Irene watched mothers with children walk along the sidewalk, an older couple come out of the dry cleaner, and then to her immediate right, was Ridley sitting at an outside bistro talking to someone she didn't know. *"Is that why he wouldn't take my call?"* Irene asked herself. Whoever he was talking to, the conversation seemed intense. Not being able to take the mystery any longer, she turned to gather her things from the back seat when there was a knock on her window.

There stood Mayor Henson. So engrossed in her snooping, Irene never saw him approach her vehicle.

He opened the door for her, and while trying to catch her breath, Irene played off her startled reaction.

"Why Mayor, your timing is impeccable as usual." She offered her hand, so he could help her out of the car.

"Not really. I was coming from the Jeweler when I saw you sitting there watching Ridley," he nudged her gently in a teasing manner.

"Why does everyone keep thinking there is something going on with me and Ridley? We are just friends. Nothing more!" Irene realized her tone was guilty after she said it.

"Maybe it's because you are trying so hard to convince us there is nothing going on," the Mayor continued teasing her.

Walking toward the Mayor's office, Irene could not help but notice the beautiful young woman who had Ridley's undivided attention.

"Well, are you going to come in, or continue to stare at Ridley?" asked the Mayor.

Once again, the Mayor broke her concentration as he held the door open for her.

"I must be losing my edge," she thought to herself. "I have to pull myself together."

"So what were you doing at the Jeweler?" Irene decided to change the subject of her and Ridley.

"Picking up Pearl's gift for Saturday night. Want to see it? Sure you do." He answered before she could respond. One thing the mayor knew was Irene did not turn down the opportunity to know something before anyone else.

"You're going to have to wait to see it with everyone on Saturday. Sorry, but it's already been wrapped." He could see the disappointment on Irene's face as he offered her a seat, he chuckled and walked around to his chair behind the desk.

A stout man, tall and still fairly handsome, Mayor Henson had been the mayor of Anna for thirty plus years. He'd worked hard to keep order and the beliefs they held sacred in check. Because Anna was a town of affluence, it wasn't hard to maintain its core values. Even if everyone didn't believe in them.

The crime was low and almost nonexistent, the towns' people were close knit. Most of the residents were second, third and some fourth generations. Anna was clean and quiet. Not much went on unless they were celebrating an event, recognizing someone, or whatever reason they could come up with to have a party. They had been fortunate enough over the years to host dignitaries who wanted a place to escape, and because Mayor Henson had been well known and connected, Anna was the chosen place for many.

"So, tell me how the plans are coming for Saturday, Irene. I want Pearl to have a memorable celebration. It should look like one of her events, without her planning it, of course. Pearl has been a huge influence in this town. I'm just sorry Doc Swanson won't be here to see it." Adjusting himself in his seat, the Mayor waited with a stern look on his face for her response. It was his *let's get down to business* look.

"The plans are coming together Mayor. "We have covered everything on your list and added a couple of surprises. I think the town will be pleased with the outcome of the celebration."

With those words, Irene gave a very cynical laugh that caused the Mayor to look at her questionably.

"Is there something going on I should know about Irene? He asked, agitated.

"You have your surprises," looking at the wrapped gift on his desk," and I have mine. Don't worry Mayor, it will be an event none of us will soon forget." The Mayor hated when Irene was cynical.

There was something different in Irene's tone that made the Mayor pause. He dismissed it on the fact that she was Pearl's best friend and knew Irene would never hurt her. But there was something there. He chose instead to make sure they were on budget even with Irene's *so-called surprises*.

"Don't worry my friend, the extras are on me. Consider them my personal contribution to the evening." Irene tried her best to reassure the Mayor.

"What are you up to Irene? This event is not one of your news stories where you can shock everyone with your element of surprise, is it? I don't want anything to undermine Saturday. Is that understood? If there is something I need to be made aware of, tell me now!" The Mayor's patience was wearing thin with Irene and her shenanigans.

His temper rose. He was not one for playing games. He was all for fun but had no time for games right now. Leaning forward in his custom mahogany nail head chair, arms resting on his antique matching desk, he eyed her square on. Irene knew she had taken things too far.

"I'm sorry Mayor, she was quick to try and clean up her behavior. I was just having fun. I promise you everything is just fine. Pearl will have the celebration she deserves."

After covering a few more details, they ended their meeting and the Mayor walked her to the front door. Walking toward her car, Irene remembered Ridley. When she looked down the now quiet sidewalk, he and his companion were gone. Her heart sank. She would have to question him about it later.

Irene made several stops before going home. One was to food shop. She wanted to set the atmosphere for Ridley to tell her what she wanted to know. She was good at planning and he hadn't seen anything yet.

Chapter 10

Pearl & The Grandchildren

Andrew and Katelyn decided they would cook dinner for Pearl and the children that evening. They banned their mother from the kitchen and after her objecting failed, Pearl decided to spend the time with the grandchildren.

She and the grands headed to the backyard and sat on the patio. They each selected a specific spot and started to engage in interesting conversation.

Jon who was extremely handsome and very well-mannered looked identical to his grandfather. Recently, he started dating and was sharing his experience with Pearl.

"Her name is Avery, she's smart and funny, and I think I really like her Gramma."

"Does she have siblings?" asked Pearl.

"A younger brother," this time Brian chimed in to answer the question. "He's ten and his name is Tristan."

As if he hadn't interrupted, Pearl continued, "How do her parents feel about you?"

"Okay, I guess. They invited me to a basketball game with them recently and to dinner a couple of times." Jon waited for his grandmother's response.

"That's a good sign. Do they allow her to come to your house at all?"

"Yes, she has been over a few times, and she gets along well with everyone, even Grace." Jon looked at Grace and squinched his nose.

"How did Grace meet her?" Pearl ignored Jon's gesture.

"Keaton and Grace stayed with us when Aunt Kate and Uncle David went out of town one weekend. They met then and became friends. Gramma, you know Grace doesn't warm up to anybody that easily!"

Jon put his arm around Grace and kissed the side of her face. She let out a scream of disgust. Punching him in the arm, Grace jumped in the conversation after the interruption of her texting.

She's okay, Gramma. I don't understand what she sees in this one though. I think she can do better." Giggling now at her cousin and hitting him with a cushion from the lawn furniture, Grace leaned against Jon and let out a huge sigh.

Pearl was enjoying the conversation and the time with her grandchildren. For a brief minute she wished her husband was alive to see how well Andrew and Katelyn had done with raising these beautiful children. Keaton brought Pearl back to reality.

"When you move Gramma, maybe Jon will bring her to meet you or maybe when you come visit."

"I would like that very much. She sounds like a lovely girl." Pearl was pleased at the thought of meeting Jon's girlfriend. It meant a lot to her.

Briefly changing the subject, Pearl stroked Brian's hair and jokingly told him he needed a haircut. He shook it like a wet dog and tousled it over his head. They all broke out in laughter. Pearl remembered Andrew at that age and shook her head. Brian was so much like his dad.

Andrew surfaced, interrupting the conversation to inform them dinner was ready. The children ran to the house to get ready for dinner. Pearl reached for Andrew's hand and when he put his hand in hers, she hugged him real tight. She was very happy.

Chapter 11

The Confrontation

Irene was cooking and singing while waiting for Ridley to come over. It was what she needed to occupy her time. Refusing to harp on how to drill him on his day when he arrived, she chose to busy herself. Besides, it had been hours since her call to him. He still had not returned it. What was going on with him and who was the woman with him? Did she really care or was she just nosey? Did she feel someone was getting something over on her? Heck for all she knew it could have been a client; he still practiced law part time. She didn't know her though. Irene knew everybody. Did the woman come in from another town? Irene went back to singing. Determined not to worry over such silliness. Soon Ridley would be there, and she would get the answers to her questions.

The evening would be special Irene decided, so dinner would be served in the dining room. Setting the table, she pulled candles from a drawer in the kitchen, gathered crystal candle holders from the cabinet while grabbing two plates from her everyday china collection. The flowers she picked up from the florist earlier were cut and placed in a crystal vase in the center of the table. The aroma that lingered in the air was an added bonus.

It wasn't long before the doorbell rang. Irene knew it was Ridley. She removed her apron, fluffed her hair, checked her appearance in the foyer mirror, and answered the door. There stood Ridley. His normal happy self, sharply dressed as always, with a devilish grin on his handsome face.

"What are you up to Ridley?" Irene blurted out after she'd looked him over. Trying to distract herself from his appearance but also trying to remain focused, she chose the gruff approach with him.

Ridley stepped inside the house, ignoring her sarcastic welcome and complimented her on the wonderful aroma coming from her kitchen.

"Are you cooking yourself Irene Pritchard, or did you have a domestic come over and do it for you? Ridley loved joking with her and seeing her get riled up.

"I will have you know I cooked this myself! I can cook you know." Irene fell right into his trap.

"I know. You very seldom do though. I am not complaining. Not one bit, just pleasantly surprised, that's all."

Ridley leaned in to give a big wet kiss and pat her butt when Irene turned toward the kitchen. Following her, he noticed the dining room table set.

"Well, what is this? Are we expecting someone else over I am not aware of?"

"Of course not, don't be ridiculous! Why would I want the gossiping town folk in my business like that? Our arrangement has worked all these years, why would I ruin it now?" Irene was testy.

"A fellow can hope you know. What are you cooking anyway? It smells good in here." Ridley sniffed the air while taking in the view of Irene's efforts.

"Thank you. She replied, a bit more mellow this time. Crab stuffed Filet mignon with roasted red potatoes and sautéed green beans with almonds. And if you behave yourself during dinner, black forest cake for dessert. But only if you behave. Now pour us a glass of wine and sit down." Irene motioned her command.

She turned her back to Ridley, not wanting him to see the smile on her face. He obliged her without another word. The two sipped from their glasses enjoying the taste in silence. After a few minutes of small talk dinner was ready to be served.

They sat down at a candlelit table and Ridley was elated that Irene had gone to all the trouble of cooking a fabulous meal just for him. But what was she up to? This was out of character for her. After a few more bites he had to know.

"Out with it! What is going on in that head of yours Irene Pritchard? I have known you long enough to know when you are up to something, or on to something. Now, which is it?" Ridley kindly rested his silverware to the sides of his plate, sat back and waited for her response.

Irene finished the food in her mouth while waiting for the appropriate response. This was not how she wanted to lead into this conversation. Raising a finger to let him know she needed a minute, she took a sip of wine.

"Did you take on a new client?" She asked.

"What?"

"Did you take on a new client?" Repeating the question.

"No. Why?"

"Is there something you want to tell me?" Irene wiped the corners of her mouth with her lace trimmed napkin.

"What do you want to know, Irene? Obviously, you want to know something, so just get to it!"

Ridley was not one for foolishness and as much as Irene liked controlling their situation she knew when he had had enough.

"I saw you today at the bistro by the Mayor's office. You obviously didn't see me as you were engrossed in your conversation."

Ridley wasn't prepared for this line of questioning. It was the last thing he thought would be on her radar.

"I am not prepared to talk to you about that just yet."

"Why not?"

"It is not something I am going to discuss with you right now. Maybe in the future, but not now Irene."

Ridley's voice was stern. Irene was now more intrigued. He never kept secrets from her. Ridley knew she didn't like it. But he wasn't going to discuss it tonight. She had to learn to deal with his answer. Stunned by it obviously, because this was not like him, Irene knew she could always investigate it if she wanted. Wait a minute, that's how the information about Savannah Jones was found out. The busyness of the day made her forget all about that. This present situation would have to wait, she had to get back to Savannah Jones and work her plan to bring the truth to light. First, she had to finish her evening with Ridley, and then call Pearl.

Chapter 12

Family

Dinner was wonderful. Katelyn and Andrew truly outdid themselves. The chicken casserole, garden salad, and garlic rolls were a huge hit, even with the kids. Andrew baked an apple pie and the kids couldn't wait to dig into it. He learned his baking skills from his mother. She'd taught him well.

Pearl sat at the table smiling at the kids as they jumped up ready to clean the kitchen when dinner was over.

"What did you promise them?" she asked Katelyn.

"Nothing. They wanted to do it. How was your time with them this afternoon?"

"It went really well. I was glad to catch up with them and see how they get along together. I also was glad to talk to Jon about Avery. I can't wait to meet her."

"I haven't met her yet, but Grace loves her. Andrew and Sharon approve of her as well. They don't want it to get too serious of course, but for now, it seems to be going well."

"What seems to be going well?" Andrew asked as he entered the dining room.

"Talking about Jon and Avery," Katelyn answered and pulled out a chair for him to join them.

"Yeah, she's a good kid. Comes from a good home, and she likes hanging out with Jon. I have of course had the "talk" with him. Sharon and I don't want it to get too serious. So far, we have no reason to worry. So, Mom, the movers are here in a week. Do you have the keys to the new place yet? We'd like to see it while we're here."

Pearl noticed the shift in conversation and felt she'd missed something but didn't press the issue. She always had an open relationship with Katelyn and Andrew and didn't believe they would hide anything from her intentionally.

"I have the keys already son. We can ride over tomorrow if you like. It's a good hour away with traffic, but still close enough where I can get back here and visit. It's going to be an adjustment, but I will get through it. This house is just too much to maintain anymore, and I look forward to being closer to you two. I like the idea of a two-and-a-half-hour distance as oppose to three and a half."

"I like the idea of you being in the same city as us," Katelyn was quick to let her know.

Andrew instantly agreed.

"We've talked about this already, Pearl said. "You all have your lives, and I still have one you know. I am active in a lot of clubs, and even though I am stepping away from planning and organizing events, there is still lots I want to do here. Besides, my friends are here. I also don't want you to alter your lives for me."

"At least you will be out of this God-awful town." Katelyn never hid her feelings about the town of Anna.

"Please let's not go down that road again, Katelyn. She's leaving, and we won't have any reason to come back here." Andrew used a tone with her Pearl hadn't heard before.

"Good!" was all Katelyn would say.

Pearl intervened in the banter between them by promising to show them the new place the next day. "Should we wait for Sharon and David to arrive?"

"No. They won't get here until late Friday," Katelyn reminded her.

David and Katelyn had been married for sixteen years. David was a surgeon and couldn't clear his schedule until Friday.

Andrew had been married to Sharon seventeen and a half years. She was a reporter working on a story and couldn't leave until Friday either. Sharon and David managed to book the same flight and would travel together, saving an additional trip to the airport for Andrew.

"They will just have to miss out on all the fun. That's the price they pay for being important people." Andrew gave his usual wink and big grin to Pearl.

Andrew was so handsome, and he reminded Pearl how much she missed their father. He was such a gentleman who apparently passed that trait on to Jon. Andrew always had a way of charming Pearl as a child. Years later and it hadn't changed.

"You and Katelyn are just as important. Don't let anyone tell you differently," Pearl assured him.

Andrew was the President of a Tech company and Katelyn designed furniture for high-end furniture stores. They both were in high demand. Pearl was pleased how their lives turned out. They lived simply despite their successes and had done a great job with raising their children.

The children came storming into the dining room with plans they made for the evening while cleaning the kitchen. They wanted to go into town to explore the arcade. They'd seen it when Andrew took them to the movies a couple of days earlier. He'd promised to take them back. As much as the adults didn't want to do it, they agreed but only for one hour.

The children wanted to negotiate more time, but Katelyn told them to take it or leave it. So, they took it.

Pearl and Katelyn grabbed their wraps, climbed into Andrew's rented SUV, along with the children and headed to town.

Andrew stayed with them while Katelyn and Pearl parked at the bistro that was still open for coffee. They talked about the latest gossip, watched the few people in town finish their shopping while they sipped their coffee. Katelyn looked around main street. It hadn't changed much over the years.

The one thing about small towns is they usually don't stay open late. By eight o'clock during the week, they are closed. For them to remain open to eleven on the weekend is a big deal in Anna. The only exception to the rule is when an event was going on and then it may go until midnight.

Laughing at the very thought if it all, Katelyn asked her mother for the first time about the details for Saturday evening.

"I don't really know. They want it to be a surprise, and Irene has not let anything slip. That's a first for her you know." The two women laughed.

"I'm sure it will be dinner, dancing, people sharing their stories of how we met or how I planned an event for them. The Mayor will say a few words and that will be it. I am not expecting anything more, honestly."

"They owe you so much more," snapped Katelyn.

"Katelyn, you must learn to forgive the past. You have so much to be thankful for and holding on to bitterness is nothing but poison to your soul. You don't want to pass that on to Grace or Keaton. They are beautiful children. Don't let them see this side of you. Love covers a multitude of faults, regardless of who makes them."

Katelyn couldn't control the emotion her mother stirred in her. Pearl had a way of doing that. As much as Katelyn tried to control it, she couldn't. Trying to bat away the tears, she finally let them fall.

"Oh, honey….. I didn't mean to make you cry. I love you so much and want to see you happy and not holding on to the past of things that will probably never change. You can only change yourself and not the opinions of others."

Pearl wiped the tears from Katelyn's face and held her hand.

"Thank you Mom, you've always seen the world differently from everybody else, and I'm glad. You've always been open with us and to the world. I think that's why everyone is drawn to you whether they realize it or not. I'm just glad Andrew and I do. I love you too." Katelyn managed to get the words out while wiping the tears that were now falling freely.

It wasn't long before the hour passed when Andrew and the kids came strolling down the sidewalk to the bistro.

"Have fun at the arcade?" Pearl asked, giving Katelyn time to recover from their talk.

The grandchildren responded in unison, "Yes!"

"Good," she said, "let's go home we have a long day tomorrow."

"What are we doing?" asked Grace.

"It's a surprise. You'll have to wait and see," Pearl told her as they climbed back into the SUV and headed home.

Chapter 13

The Plan

Irene woke the next morning eager to plan her day. Before getting out of bed, she propped herself up against her white goose down Egyptian cotton pillows, covered in Supima cotton cases. Thinking of her conversation with Ridley the night before, it was hard to believe he was keeping something from her. She chose to let it go. Leading him to think she was willing to wait until he was ready to talk about it. Irene had gone on with the evening as if everything was okay. Ridley was none the wiser. When she was ready to end the evening early, he'd wanted to stay longer. Insisting she was tired from a long day and in need of rest, Irene was adamant. Although Ridley did the dishes, Irene refused to let him stay. She simply wanted to retire early. Alone. He didn't argue and soon went home. Promising herself to find out what it was, after things were over with Pearl. She wouldn't show any concern toward him at all. That's what made her a good reporter.

Feeling she had spent enough time thinking about something she could not change, Irene made her bed, showered, and started her day. Her to-do list was long and there was very little time to complete it. Pearl usually would be a big help with things like this, but not this time. Irene would have to get out of her haze of conniving and get to work.

Before long she'd made her way to town. Her first stop was the printer to approve the programs. From there it was the bakery, the florist and the jeweler. Irene was so busy she'd forgotten to eat lunch. It was the slight pounding in her left temple that reminded her. Stopping briefly to grab a sandwich from the nearby diner, Irene finished the to-do list and headed home. It was on the drive home that she had time to think about her news. Thinking carefully on how to deliver it, she had to plan it well. As bizarre as the news was, she would have a hard time convincing everyone, so it had to be a solid plan. Playing different scenarios over in her head while she drove helped Irene plot the perfect plan.

Chapter 14

The Adventure

When Pearl woke the next morning, the grandchildren were already up, dressed and ready to go on their adventure. Not knowing what it was, didn't stop them from being excited and ready. Pearl, unaware she'd over slept felt bad that everyone was waiting on her. When she dressed, went downstairs, several flower deliveries and gifts had been couriered over. Katelyn had taken a list of messages from well-wishers all excited about the celebration.

Andrew rose to greet her as she entered the breakfast room and pulled out a chair for her. "Sit here, my queen," he said as he kissed her cheek.

"Thank you, my prince," Pearl smiled as she sat. Forgive my tardiness, I had no idea it was this late.

"Don't worry about it, you must have needed the rest, and we certainly were not going to disturb the queen," said Andrew jokingly to her.

Katelyn brought a breakfast plate to Pearl, along with a hot cup of coffee.

While she ate, Katelyn went over the messages, talked about the flowers and couldn't wait to see the gifts Pearl received.

"That will have to wait," Pearl told them. She didn't want to keep the grandchildren waiting any longer than necessary. They needed to get on the road. Pearl was excited for them to see her new place. She'd fallen in love with it and hoped they would like it also.

On the drive to Meadowdale, Pearl sang songs with the kids and played games. Although the older kids thought it was lame, they participated in the activities. She had done the same with Katelyn and Andrew whenever they'd taken road trips. Before long, they'd arrived at the new place.

When they pulled into the driveway aligned with evergreens, it was a far cry from the house they were raised in, but still a nice home.

"Well, what do you think?" Pearl asked as they got out of the truck and stood in the driveway.

The grandchildren didn't hesitate to go around back to check things out.

"It's nice," Katelyn said, hesitantly.

"Nice? Is that all you have to say? Let's go inside and I will show you nice." Pearl pulled her by the hand.

After searching for her key, Pearl opened the door and they went inside. Neither Katelyn or Andrew was prepared for what they saw. The beautiful hardwood floors, the marble countertops, the double trey ceilings, the boxwood moldings, the travertine tile in the bathrooms, and the breathtaking back view from the palladium windows, all blew them away. Granted it was not their childhood home, but this was better than they expected.

There is still plenty of room for you when you visit, Pearl assured them as they toured the house. With four bedrooms as opposed to the seven she was leaving, nobody would be cramped. She made plans with her decorator to turn the bonus room into a space specifically for the grandchildren.

"Mom, you don't have to do that. Use that space as you see fit, don't waste it on the kids," Katelyn said still taking in the view of the house.

"I am using it as I see fit. I want them to feel at home when they come. Besides, I won't have to climb those stairs every day to get something. Whatever I need can be put on the first floor. Maybe they will come more often." Pearl smiled as she said it.

"I don't think that will ever be a problem with them. They all love being around you," Katelyn said relieving any doubt.

When the grandchildren came in Pearl sent them upstairs to view the bonus room. Explaining to them how the room was for them. Their assignment was to come up with ideas on how they would like it to look. She would give the plan to her decorator to execute. The one rule was each must have a say in the planning, or the final decision would be hers. They would have to live with it.

Pearl, Katelyn, and Andrew stepped on the back patio and realized how amazing the new property was. There was a retaining wall where spider plants decorated the top, a beautiful teak bridge that crossed a man-made pond, a stone firepit surrounded with six adirondack chairs, immaculate landscaping, and a raised deck with wrought iron spindles.

"I plan to spend a lot of time out here," Pearl said breaking the silence.

"I see why," Andrew said, "this is perfect."

"I have to agree," Katelyn chimed in, "this is breathtaking."

"I knew you would like it once you saw it. I think it is perfect for me." Pearl closed her eyes recapturing the view.

"This is still a bit large for you Mom, are you sure this is not too much to maintain?" Andrew asked.

"I've already talked to someone who will come once a week to clean. There's a lawn service I've hired to maintain this gorgeous yard. I will be fine. Don't worry about me. I can't wait to move in. We just have to get through this weekend first."

"Are you sure you don't want us to help you?" Andrew seemed quite concerned.

"Oh gosh no, Andrew. Thank you. The movers have it all under control. Besides, you need to get your family back and get on with your lives. This will be fine."

"I think we should probably check on the children," Katelyn interrupted the conversation, "I haven't seen any of them for a while. I'm going to make sure they are okay."

You worry too much. What could they possibly get into? They are not toddlers and there is nothing in there." Pearl teased Katelyn knowing she would head toward the house anyway.

"I think I would feel better making sure." Turning to go back toward the house Katelyn ignored Andrew and Pearl's laughter over her protection of the children; who were no longer children.

When Pearl and Andrew finally returned to the house, the children were still upstairs planning what they wanted the bonus room to look like. Katelyn standing in the doorway eavesdropping on their conversation, didn't hear Pearl or Andrew approach right away. When they saw her standing there they looked at each other shaking their heads.

"This is what she rushed back for? To stand and spy on the kids. Weirdo!" Andrew rolled his eyes while walking off.

Pearl laughed at his never- ending sense of humor especially when it came to giving his sister a hard time. Katelyn gave him the usual sister punch in the arm. Pearl pushed past them both and went in with the grandchildren.

"This is interesting," Pearl told them. Sitting on the floor with them she looked at the rough sketch Jon drew.

"It is." Jon spoke for the group. He shared how each of them wanted something different but nothing outrageous or expensive, and they'd manage to agree without fighting or name calling. Pearl said how proud she was of them. Andrew told them to wrap it up if they wanted lunch. He didn't have to do much convincing. The grands agreed they could finish the discussion later, and submit their request to their grandmother in writing. Pearl was very impressed at their level of maturity.

The choice for lunch was a Mexican restaurant on the drive back. Three of the kids slept most of the way while Pearl, Katelyn and Andrew talked about ideas for the house.

Before long they arrived home. The front porch was covered with several deliveries of flowers and gifts.

"They won't stop coming. Is this what we have to look forward to for the next two days?" Andrew teased, "You must really be somebody in this town."

"She is," Katelyn chimed in before Pearl could answer, "she is a Queen....our queen, and she deserves every bit of this attention and more. I can't wait to see what Saturday night has in store." She locked arms with her mother from the car to the front door. Each person grabbed a package or flower and brought it inside. It was the only way to get in the door. Once inside they had to deal with the never-ending phone messages.

While Pearl listened to messages from well-wishers, Katelyn handled the gifts. Enlisting the help of Grace, the gifts were logged and before they realized how much time had passed it was nearing dinner. Andrew and the boys had taken it upon themselves to start it. The females were grateful.

Chapter 15

Secrets

"I think I may have to tell Irene the truth about you," Ridley said to the woman on the other end of the phone. "I knew it was a mistake for you to come here. It was a huge risk, but I never expected her to see us together."

"Can you say I'm a client without having to tell her the truth. I don't want you to jeopardize everything you've worked so hard for." The voice on the other end sounding concerned.

"She is going to know sooner or later. If I tell her you are a client and she finds out the truth, it will be disastrous. She is a reporter, so I'm not sure how much she has delved into my past already. Irene may know and is just waiting for me to tell her. Either way, it is not going to go well. There is a strong chance I will have to leave Anna before it's all over. I am prepared if I must, but I have made a good living here, along with good friends." Ridley's voice sounded disappointed.

"Promise me you won't tell her until after the dinner on Saturday. Don't do anything to take from Mrs. Swanson's evening ." The voice still sounding concerned.

"Okay. I promise, I will tell her after the dinner. But in the meantime, I think you shouldn't come back here until after I tell her." His voice was filled with caution.

"Agreed. I love you."

"I love you too. I will call you tomorrow."

Chapter 16

Deception

Irene spent the day working on her "To-do" list and didn't have much time to think about her plan. Between the Mayor, the florist, numerous phone calls from people with last minute questions; she'd been busy. She was ready to go home, have a glass of wine and collect her thoughts. Everything had to be perfect. She couldn't let anyone think otherwise because the impact of her news had to be significant. She reminded herself to call Pearl since they hadn't spoken all day. Irene was sure Pearl was busy with Katelyn and Andrew, so she would be off the hook for not calling sooner.

As Irene drove through the streets of Anna, she appreciated the town even more. How the residents maintained their standard of living. How it hadn't been corrupted by the big city and the people for the most part, were honest and trustworthy.

The streets were clean, the lawns meticulously manicured, homes well maintained. It was the American dream. Irene was glad to be a resident of this fine town and wouldn't let outsiders corrupt it. She would see to it if it was the last thing she did.

Arriving home, she put away her packages, changed into more comfortable clothes, poured herself a glass of wine and sat in her favorite chair.

"Ahh….this feels nice," she said aloud. Closing her eyes to inhale the aroma of the Merlot and exhale the cares of the day, she smiled to herself. Irene was a woman with a secret, but in a couple of days, everyone would know it.

Remembering to call Pearl, she opened her eyes, grabbed the phone from the coffee table and made the call.

"Hi Pearl, how was your day? Are you enjoying your time with your family?" She asked questions without waiting for answers.

"Yes. We went over to see the house, and they loved it. I feel better moving now knowing Katelyn and Andrew are okay with it. What did you do today?" Pearl asked.

"Just ran errands for Saturday. I think you will be pleased with what we have planned. It is going to be the event of the year!" Irene genuinely sounded excited.

"I told you before, I don't want you all to go overboard. A simple dinner is alright with me," Pearl reminded her.

"Nonsense! We want to make sure we send you out with everything you deserve. You have impacted so many people's lives. It is the least we can do." Irene made a face as she said the words. Her horns were starting to show. Good thing Pearl was on the phone and not talking to her face to face.

"Are you getting excited?" Irene asked Pearl.

"A bit. Flowers, cards, and gifts have been coming in from all over, not to mention the phone calls. Good thing the children are here to help me deal with it. It's starting to get a little overwhelming now."

"Good thing. They can see first-hand the impact you've had on the town since they've been gone. And, what did you expect, *Miss Social Coordinator*? You had to know this was coming." Irene was sounding a bit sarcastic.

Pearl disregarded Irene's sarcasm. "What are you doing with your evening? Why don't you come over and join us for dinner?"

"I can't tonight. I'm just getting in and I am tired. Besides, I have more phone calls to make and I want to turn in early." Irene checked her call list as she said it.

"Old man Ridley isn't coming over, is he?"

"I have told you for years there is nothing going on between me and old man Ridley. That's all in your head!" The agitation was growing in Irene's voice.

Laughing at Irene's obvious agitation, Pearl changed the subject to an invitation for dinner the following evening. "Sharon and David will be here by then and you can see everybody before the dinner on Saturday. I won't take no for an answer," Pearl insisted.

"I will let you know tomorrow for sure by noon if that's okay. I'm not sure when I will be through with everything. I will try my best to be done for dinner." Irene promised with no plans of keeping it.

"Okay, I'm going to hold you to it."Reminding Irene of her expectation.

"Okay Pearl,"was all Irene said. The ladies ended the call.

Before Irene could put the phone on the cradle and remove her hand, it rang. It was Ridley.

"Hello," was what Irene heard from his deep husky voice on the other end.

"Hello." Irene was always glad to hear the sound of that voice on the phone; she just didn't want him to know it.

"Have you had dinner yet?" Ridley asked.

"No. Just got home about forty-five minutes ago and was too tired to stop."

"Good. I'll pick us up something and see you in thirty."

Before Irene could object he'd hung up. "Fine, she thought to herself. We can talk about this person he doesn't want to talk about when he gets here."

Irene got up from her comfortable chair, showered and slipped into a simple floral dress. She set the table and waited for Ridley to arrive.

It wasn't long before the sound of the garage door opened. Irene knew Ridley had arrived. He had honored her request of parking in the garage to keep the neighbors out of her business. It worked since no one other than Pearl ever said anything to her. Besides, she had so much dirt on a lot of people in town they wouldn't dare talk about her personal life.

Ridley came through the kitchen door, planted a big wet kiss right on her lips, sat the bags on the table and unpacked their dinner. He'd stopped at Oliver's, the best restaurant in Anna and ordered Irene's favorite prime rib with Oliver's famous horseradish sauce, perfectly steamed asparagus spears and garlic roasted baby potatoes. She was pleased with his choice. He ordered for himself a Black Angus New York strip, au gratin potatoes and roasted brussel sprouts. He also had a bottle of Cabernet Sauvignon to top it off. The two plated their food and sat down to dinner.

"So what did you do today?" Ridley broke the silence.

"I met with the Mayor, the florist, the band, made sure the car would be on time to get Pearl. You know Diane over at the jeweler is making me wait until Saturday morning to pick up Pearl's gift? The nerve of that woman. I think sometimes she has it in for me. Maybe it's because I broke the story of her husband's extracurricular activity with Beverly Winston under the guise of *"planning."* Irene made sure to use air quotes for effect.

Ridley loved a lot of things about Irene, but this was not one of them. He did not like how the "reporter" in her could destroy the lives of many people, and be okay with it. Irene had delivered excellent reporting over the years, but the last few of her career were horrible. Ridley was sure that's why the studio was "moving in another direction." It was their way, he believed, of giving her the boot but allowing her to maintain some dignity. There were still people in town who avoided her when they saw her coming. Beyond that one thing, and her pride, Irene was a wonderful woman. He had fallen in love with her. For years, Ridley wanted to make their relationship public, but she wouldn't hear of it. He chose to oblige her hoping Irene would change her mind. She had not.

"What did your day look like?" Her question brought him back to the present.

"I had an easy day today. Mostly paperwork and filings, a few phone calls and I played a round of golf with the Mayor." Ridley paused, taking a sip of wine.

"Really, I saw him earlier today, and he didn't say anything about playing golf." Irene wondered if Ridley was being truthful.

"Why would he discuss golf with you? He knew you wouldn't be the least bit interested," He laughed.

"You are correct. I absolutely don't have any interest."

"Eat up. I have a surprise for you." Ridley pointed to her food with his fork.

"What is it? You know I hate surprises," Irene stopped eating.

"I know. But you will like this one and it's not threatening. I promise," Ridley assured her.

When they finished their dinner, he cleared the plates and put them in the sink to soak. Ridley wanted to give Irene her surprise. First was her favorite dessert. The decadent Red Velvet trifle, he'd left in the bag for the perfect time. What Irene didn't know, but was about to find out, Ridley was about to propose.

Never one to turn down dessert, Irene was thrilled it was something simple. Not sure if she could handle anything major right now. But then it happened. Ridley sat next to her, grabbed her free hand and began:

"Irene, we have been doing this thing now for over twenty years. You know how I feel about you and you must feel something toward me, otherwise, we wouldn't keep doing this. I want to be able to walk down the street with you, park in the driveway and not just the garage, like I'm a fugitive. I am at a point in my life where I want commitment. I love you. I want to spend whatever time we have left together. So, I am asking you to stop this nonsense, and let's get married while we can both walk down the aisle." Ridley reached into his pocket and pulled out a three-carat platinum cushion shaped ring.

Irene was stunned at this proposal but not surprised. She knew how Ridley felt about her, and she had put him off for years. Feeling like a whirlwind just came through the room and swallowed her up, Irene didn't know what to say. Having played this game with him so long, not wanting to admit there was something about Ridley that made her want to be with him. If her pride would let her go long enough, maybe she'd admit she loved him too. There were many thoughts flying through Irene's mind. *How would she even begin to explain this to people? She had denied the rumors for years and wanted to believe she had pulled it off. What would her life look like to be married? The only marriage she had ever known was to her career as a reporter. She wouldn't allow herself to be tied to anyone or anything but the next story. She wanted desperately to say yes, but there were so many things to talk about. The main thing being the woman she saw him with a few days earlier that he didn't want to talk about. She would have to know the answer to that mystery. Then there was this business with Pearl that she must finish before she could think about moving on to anything else. She knew he was waiting for a response, and needed to say something. He had just placed her in a position to be vulnerable and that went against her tough exterior. But, he was handsome with his wavy hair that had the right mix of gray to it and those hazel eyes that always melted her heart every time she looked into them.*

"Why do you want to go and mess up what we have?,"was all Irene managed to say.

Prepared for the resistance, Ridley was quick to answer her.

"Woman, I just told you why, and if you get out of your pride long enough, you would agree this is the next move. It is time. Unless I have misread the signals all these years and this is not what you want, I am willing to end this now. Right now. I want someone to grow old with, wake up with every day, share my innermost secrets and fears with. I am tired of this charade. I want more. So if you don't, you have to tell me right now." There was no mistaking Ridley's intention.

Irene never experienced his sternness before. With his clients, maybe, but never with her.

"So, is this what my life is going to be like going forward? You dictating to me how things are going to be?" She tried to deflect from the seriousness of the moment.

"Is that your way of saying *yes*?" Ridley refused to give in to her now.

"Well, when you put it like that what choice do I have?" Irene looked at him, wanting so desperately to change the subject. Knowing Ridley was serious and it wasn't an option.

"You have to say it. For once, I am not going to let you skirt around this. If you want to marry me you have to say it.

With butterflies fluttering in her stomach and fighting back tears to force out one simple word, Irene finally heard herself say what she thought she never would to a man.

"Yes."

Chapter 17

Memory Lane

David and Sharon were glad to see Katelyn and Andrew when they arrived at the airport. Due to some cancellations they both were able to take an earlier flight. Their spouses were delighted at the news. The children wanted to come along, but Pearl convinced them to stay with her and help sort through mail and gifts that were still pouring in. She promised them afterwards they would bake cookies and make their favorite peach ice cream from her secret recipe. It was only after that Katelyn and Andrew were able to leave without them.

David and Katelyn sat in the back seat. David holding her hand immediately noticed the tension radiating from his wife.

"So how's it been being back in the great town of Anna?"David asked.

"We are making the best of it," Andrew answered from the driver's seat. "I am proud of Katelyn for making the effort."

"I can't believe you guys grew up here," Sharon chimed in, "I mean it looks like a wonderful place to live from the outside, but the history of it really makes it kind of creepy. You wouldn't think people still believe the things this town was founded on."

"I'm just glad Mom is finally moving away from here." Katelyn meant every word of that statement. She wished it would have been a lot sooner.

"Just think this time next month she will be out and you won't have to think about this town ever again." David was trying his best to reassure his wife, but he knew the impact the town had on her. Until she came back to this place, Katelyn was a fun, loving and caring person. Being back here made her guarded and tense, and he didn't like to see this side of his wife.

They rode for a while in silence. Finally Sharon asked about the kids and how they'd occupied their time. Katelyn and Andrew told them about the arcade, them helping with dinner, cleaning the kitchen and the time with their grandmother. They laughed at how Pearl made them helpers with sorting the mail and gifts in exchange for cookies and homemade ice cream.

Andrew made Sharon aware of Pearl's knowledge of Avery. "What exactly does she know? And how?" Sharon sounding almost frantic.

"When they were spending time out on the patio with her, Jon brought it up. I think all she knows is they're friends. Besides, Mom is not like that. She will accept anyone. If she knew more she would have said something," Andrew told her.

"I just want to know what to say and not say around her." Sharon was glad Pearl knew about Avery. She knew how Jon felt about her and his grandmother. It must have been real important for him to share it with her.

"Mom will be okay. Just don't bring Avery around while Mom is still here." Katelyn just had to add that to the conversation.

"Don't worry. It will be long after her move," Sharon replied.

They all laughed.

Katelyn went on to tell Sharon about the new house and the plans Pearl had for it. Especially the plans for the children to have the upper floor when they visited. Even down to the decorating. Each child could add their own special touch.

"I always thought your mother was one special lady," David added. "Who would give up space in their home for children she only gets to see a few times a year. That is special."

"Well, when you think about it, they love to go where she is, regardless of the space. I don't think they care if it's a different setting," Andrew reminded them.

"That's true," David agreed. "Technically, we could all have our own room in the house she's in now. I still can't believe you guys grew up there."

They soon arrived in Anna and silence fell between them again. Passing the manicured lawns that laid like carpet and the well-kept homes was like looking at a spread in House Beautiful magazine. It was unbelievable how immaculate the town appeared on the surface. But the dark and ugly secrets told a different story for those who knew it.

"You don't think about it growing up. You just live knowing you have great parents that love you and want the best for you. Yes, with dad being the doctor and Mom always planning something, we knew they were important, but to us, they were just mom and dad. They were so down to earth with us we didn't know any better until years later. You have to remember everybody lived well. It was normal for us. Andrew and I were involved in so many things, I don't think we noticed or understood." Katelyn was trying to explain to David.

"When did you know things were different here?" Sharon asked without thinking. Andrew squeezed Sharon's hand as a reminder that it was a subject he or Katelyn rarely liked talking about. Katelyn was grateful for the timing because they'd finally arrived at their mother's house.

Pearl met them at the door. The children didn't realize their parents had arrived. Glad to see Sharon and David, Pearl greeted them individually with long hugs and a kiss to their cheek. She had a way of making anybody feel at home. They were always glad to be in her presence.

"Come on into the kitchen. I have fresh squeezed lemonade waiting for you. I knew you would be thirsty. Lunch will be ready soon. They each took a seat at the marble top island centered in the kitchen. Each pouring their own glass of lemonade from the pitcher; Pearl brought freshly baked orange cranberry bread from the oven.

"Oh, this bread is wonderful!" Sharon remarked after taking the first bite.

"Thanks, Sharon, I knew you would like it. I had you in mind when I made it."

"What about the rest of us?" Andrew winked and gave Pearl that devilish smile.

"I knew the rest of you would eat whatever I put in front of you." She slapped Andrew with the hand towel. "Now don't eat too much bread. Lunch is just about ready."

It wasn't long before the children realized the adults were back and bombarded the kitchen. After the hugs and pleasantries, they all sat down to a carefully selected lunch of stuffed chicken breast, cranberry and rotini pasta salad drizzled with a honey glaze. They laughed and talked through lunch. The children told their parents how they each had a task to help Gramma with all her gifts, and how they were going to bake cookies and make homemade ice cream. Pearl knew it was also a way of reminding her they hadn't forgotten her promise to them.

"Yes, we are going to bake cookies and make homemade ice cream," Pearl confirmed.

"Then we will clean the kitchen for you so you can get ready." Andrew had already stood to clear the table before Pearl could object as he knew she would. David stood and followed suit. Katelyn grabbed the linen from the table to take it to the laundry room. Sharon went to get up and Pearl asked her to sit with her for a minute. She moved to a seat closer to Pearl without hesitation.

"How have you been? You look fabulous." Pearl was always complimenting Sharon. She'd been pleased at Andrew's choice in marriage. Sharon had never disappointed her.

"I am doing really well. How are you doing with everybody making a fuss over you? Are you excited about tomorrow night? I know we all are." Sharon smiled at her mother-in-law.

"Part of me is really excited, the other part wants it all to be over. You know I am the one who likes fussing over everybody, not the other way around. I'll have to show you what's been sent over in the last few days, it is unbelievable. I'm really glad the grands helped out with organizing it all. I've used the library to store everything for now. Maria was going to come by later today and help, but I thought this would be a great project for me and the grands."

"I would love to see it. I can only imagine what you've received. I know the children loved helping you. You are all they talk about. They value their relationship with you."

Just then the door bell rang. "I'll get it," yelled Andrew, "It's probably another delivery." Sure enough, it was. This time, it was a beautiful bouquet of white roses from the Mayor. Two dozen of the most gorgeous roses you could imagine. Perfectly arranged in a Waterford crystal vase and tied with a red and white bow trimmed in gold. Fresh, healthy flowers, fragrantly aromatic instantly engulfing the room as Andrew brought the arrangement to the table. Replacing the centerpiece on the table with the one in his hand. Pearl instructed him to place the old one on the breakfast table.

"Is this the first of the flowers?" asked Sharon.

"Goodness no!" Katelyn shouted entering the dining room. "Come with me and let me show you the sunroom. You have no idea how many deliveries have been made over the last couple of days. I don't think we had these many flowers when Dad died." Katelyn smiled back at Pearl. "She is an amazing woman if I do say so myself."

Katelyn and Sharon headed toward the sunroom. Pearl called for the grands to start their project together while David and Andrew carried luggage upstairs and sat out on the upper deck.

Chapter 18

Irene

Irene had said yes to Ridley's proposal, but, she put stipulations on her answer. Neither could say anything to anybody until after Pearl's celebration, and he had to explain the woman with him in town. He agreed Pearl shouldn't have anything interrupt her day. They both were on the same page in their thinking.

Irene couldn't believe she was going to be married. They both agreed a small simple ceremony would be best for them since neither one had any real family to speak of. They would ask the Mayor to preside over the ceremony and they would need witnesses. Irene couldn't spend time thinking about that right now, she had more pressing things to attend to and make sure the night went off without a hitch. This would truly be the night Anna would never forget, and she would be the one to deliver the news.

Irene busied herself with the final details for the day. She'd gone over her checklist one final time to make sure nothing was omitted. From the final seating arrangements, the car to pick Pearl up, checking in with the caterers for the time to serve, to the Mayor to make sure he arrived on time. The night had to be flawless. She would have to leave soon for her appointment at the spa where she would meet Pearl, Katelyn and Sharon. Having missed the dinner the night before, it was important to make the spa date. After the evening with Ridley and finalizing plans, she just couldn't make it. Pearl didn't like it but understood Irene's unavailability. Besides, it was all being done for her. Irene wanted the night to be memorable.

On the way to the spa, she received a call from the caterer regarding Pearl's cake. It wasn't something to be rectified over the phone, so Irene had to cancel with Pearl once again to tend to the crisis at hand. Relieved for the distraction, she hadn't seen Pearl since her discovery and wasn't sure if things hadn't just worked out for the best. The crisis wasn't as severe as Irene thought, she wrestled with joining the ladies at the spa or skipping it all together.

Ridley knew how close Irene was to Pearl and never wanted to come between the two. He didn't have a problem with Irene's request to wait until the celebration was over to announce their engagement. The second request was going to be harder to explain, and he wasn't sure how Irene would react. Ridley knew the unspoken rule in Anna. He knew it when he first came. The opportunity for him outweighed the weight of this antiquated town, and he'd learn to live with it. When the time came to connect with old friends Ridley would simply leave Anna to do so. Never expecting Irene to see him with "her," he now had to tell her the truth. Knowing it wasn't a good idea for "her" to come there, he figured if the question arose, he would pass "her" off as a client. It would probably cost him everything in Anna, but he was willing to take the chance. His hope was, love would supersede. He would soon find out how wrong he was.

Chapter 19

The Spa

When the ladies arrived at the spa, Katelyn was glad Irene was called away. Disappointed when she came a few minutes later, they exchanged pleasantries but Katelyn gave Irene the usual *I will hug you, but I don't trust you* look. She never liked how Irene spent years destroying lives. Katelyn hadn't been impressed with the headliners Irene interviewed either because it never made up for the people she squashed like bugs. She'd promised her mother she would tolerate Irene since it was Pearl's day.

While the ladies waited to be escorted back to the changing area, it gave Pearl and Irene a chance to catch up.

"I feel like I haven't seen you all week," Pearl admitted to her friend.

"Well, it's been a busy week, trying to get everything ready just for you."

"It doesn't change the fact that I've missed talking to you or seeing you this week," Pearl added.

"Sometimes, Pearl, you just have to roll with it." Irene snapped before realizing it.

"What does that mean? Why are you so grumpy today? I'm guessing you haven't seen Ridley this week either?" Pearl teased.

Jumping up like a spoiled school girl, Irene raised her voice. "I am really tired of you bringing up Ridley!"

The outburst had everybody's attention, even Katelyn's.

"Is everything alright over here? Katelyn asked, giving Irene an evil look.

Yes, Katelyn, everything is fine," Pearl tried to put her concern at ease. She wasn't buying Pearl's answer and asked the question a different way. "What's going on over here, Irene?"

"Oh, nothing Katelyn. I guess I'm more tired than I was willing to admit." Irene was lying, and Katelyn knew it. "I am sure I will feel better after the spa." Irene was trying hard to convince her. The last thing she wanted was to contend with Katelyn. Pearl, Irene felt she could handle, but Katelyn.......

"Ladies, we are ready for you." The masseuse interrupted the conversation. The ladies followed her back to a room setup with four tables. The lights were dim, with the smell of sandalwood and vanilla penetrating the air. The music was calming, just what they all needed. Katelyn was the last one to take her place on the table. She wanted to make sure Irene Pritchard wasn't up to something. It was hard for Katelyn to relax at first, but Marta's hands were magical and before long, she'd released the tension caused by Irene and the town of Anna. Katelyn was in complete Zen mode.

Chapter 20

The Dinner

T he day of the Recognition dinner honoring Pearl finally arrived. It wasn't a good day for Pearl though. From the time she woke that morning, she didn't feel her normal bubbly self. Something was wrong, she didn't know what, but her gut instinct sensed something was off. The uneasiness remained with her and she rarely felt that way. Trying to shake the feeling she went about her day. After last minute shopping with Katelyn and Sharon, followed by a quick lunch in town, they started to get ready for the evening.

Pearl made several failed attempts throughout the day to reach Irene. It wasn't like her to be scarce in her visits or calls, but Pearl had enjoyed the time with her family and hadn't noticed the scarceness until now.

Her uneasiness still lingered. Pearl finally chalked it up to jitters. How she loved celebrating and recognizing others, but not so much for herself. Maybe after a hot shower she would be more relaxed and could better ready herself.

The shower helped some, but her instincts were rarely off, and they were telling her something wasn't right. Pearl pushed passed the feeling and dressed for the evening. Carefully applying her makeup and styling her hair she sat and stared at the woman in the mirror. *"Hello old friend. Age has caught up with you, but you are still a beautiful woman. People love you. More importantly you have the love and support of your family. Don't worry. Things have worked to your favor. You have achieved much and now is not the time to doubt anything."* Pearl's thoughts were interrupted by a knock on the door. It was Katelyn coming to give her a hand. Pearl tried to play off the worry she felt but Katelyn knew her mother well.

"Mother, is everything okay? You've seemed a bit distracted today."

"I'm fine Katelyn," Pearl tried to reassure her.

"I don't believe you. You know you can talk to me about anything. Has Irene said or done something, because I swear mother, that woman…!"

"Stop Katelyn." Pearl grabbed her hands, looking her directly in the eyes. "Everything is fine. There is nothing for you to be concerned about." Changing the subject because she knew

Katelyn disliked Irene and would have a few words with her if she suspected Irene was the reason for her concern.

"You look amazing," Pearl complimented Katelyn on her dress. Her choice for the evening was a black cocktail dress with one open shoulder that was attached by a lace and rhinestone choker. The rhinestones played off the color of her honey brown eyes. The dress flattered her figure.

Katelyn was aware of her mother changing the subject but didn't want to do anything to spoil her evening.

"Thank you mother. I hoped it would be appropriate for the occasion. Now enough about me. Let's get you dressed, according to Irene the car should be here at 5:30. That doesn't give us much time."

"I was just finishing my makeup when you came in. I only need to slip into my dress. How does my makeup look? Did I do a good job?" Pearl turned from side to side allowing her daughter to see her complete face.

"You are as beautiful as ever. Come, let me help you with your dress." Pearl slipped into a black & silver chiffon dress with a black satin band at the waist. She slid on two-tone black and silver sling back shoes and had just enough time to put on her jewelry before Andrew knocked on the door. As the three made their way down the stairs, the rest of the family were waiting in the foyer, anticipating Pearl's debut. When Pearl reached the bottom of the stairs, looking at the grandchildren, David, then Sharon, her heart was full. This was what most people dreamed of. She happened to be living it, right in this moment. Pearl took time to compliment each one on how handsome or beautiful they were. The door bell rang. The driver along with the photographer stood at the door. After a few pictures of the family, they settled into the limo and headed to town.

The ride to the event was smooth and uneventful. The night was warm with just a hint of honeysuckle filling the air. Conversation was to a minimal. Pearl wasn't sure why but wished someone would say or do something to keep her mind from thinking about the uneasiness she continued to feel. It wasn't long before they reached their destination. The driver helped each one from the car and the red carpet was waiting for them to walk into the building.

###

Irene spent her afternoon preparing for the evening in a different way. The latest update she received confirmed her suspicion about Savannah Jones. She could hardly wait to tell the town the news. To have this knowledge and expose it meant she would be taken seriously again. For Irene refused to be the aging journalist who'd been replaced by younger blood. It would give her the respect and dignity that had been snatched from her. This would be the story of the year. Better than any other story she'd reported. Once it was revealed, Anna would never be the same and would be ever indebted to her.

Time passed quickly. Consumed by the news, Irene realized she must hurry to make the event on time. For once she couldn't be late. After a quick shower, Irene put on her makeup, got dressed and left.

The guests arrived early. No one wanted to miss the festivities. They made their way in and found their designated seats. Looking over the entire room, no expense was spared. From fine china, crystal stemware, the finest linens, not to mention, the table decorations with pink and white roses in tall crystal vases, the committee exceeded their goal. The outcome was fabulous, and everyone was talking about it. A five-piece ensemble provided the perfect music for the evening. Even in the midst of such a beautiful setting, Pearl couldn't help but wonder where Irene was. It wasn't like her to avoid the spotlight. Pearl hadn't seen her once so far. Did something happen to her friend? Surely not, she thought, or someone would have told her. Pearl and her family were seated at the head table facing the stage. A long rectangular table beautifully adorned, played off the color scheme of pink and white from the other round tables.

The place was at capacity. Several people approached Pearl to congratulate her, also to find out her future plans. It wasn't long before Irene took the stage. Pearl was relieved to know she was alright. It still bothered her that she hadn't heard from her all day though. Irene spoke in her usual professional tone. She welcomed the crowd and went over the agenda for the evening. It promised to be a momentous occasion. She introduced each dignitary as they took the stage. Each one offered the highest accolades for Pearl's achievements and contributions. Hearing speech after carefully planned speech along with laughter and grand applause, Pearl still could not shake the feeling of uneasiness.

Dinner was served. The five courses were carefully planned as the evening itself. No one complained about any of the food choices. After the clearing of the dinner dishes, dessert would be served. Irene and the Mayor were next on the program to give their speeches and presentations. It also allowed time to digest the food that had been elegantly served.

Irene took the stage again. Standing there looking over the crowd, she was dressed in a two-piece black and white crepe satin dress with a correlating jacket. As she stood at the podium waiting to speak Pearl noticed there was something different about her. Irene would not look at her friend. Pearl knew something was wrong. She could not imagine for the life of her what it could possibly be. Irene began her speech:

"Hello again. As you are fully aware we are here tonight to honor Pearl Swanson. Pearl has contributed much to our community over the last 40 years. Whether it was fundraising, planning formal dinners or simple potlucks, she shared her gift with us all. We all can agree she has brought a lot to our town.

I met Pearl about 50 years ago shortly after she came to Anna. We instantly became friends. We have shared everything together, our hopes, our dreams, our fears, and our secrets...or so I thought.

It turns out no matter how much you think you know a person, there is always something yet to be uncovered. It is without question Pearl is a very talented woman."

Irene paused, still looking at everyone but Pearl.

"Before today, I would have told you Pearl Swanson was the best friend you could ever have…," she paused again, taking a deep breath, and finally continues.

"But I have learned that she is not. Pearl Swanson is nothing more than a liar, a manipulator, a con-woman, and a deceiver. Honor her if you will – (another pause) but before you do, make sure you know who you are honoring. Ladies and gentlemen, I present to you Pearl Swanson, or should I say Savannah Jones – a black Negro woman who has lived here uninvited and has deceived us all!

The gasps across the room came in unison. The spotlight landed on Pearl. The whispers began. Her children, grandchildren, friends, neighbors, all now knew her secret. This was it, the uneasiness Pearl felt all day. It was crystal clear to her why Irene had avoided her. But how did she know?

Andrew and Katelyn looked at Pearl. Pearl unsure of what to do, stood to leave. Shaking accompanied by a shortness of breath, she collapsed to the floor. Lying there sweaty and unable to breathe, the crowd around her stood in shock. David rushed to Pearl's side. Checking her pulse and listening to her heart, he looked at Katelyn. "She's in distress. I'm not sure what exactly is happening. We must get her to the hospital immediately."

"Call 9-1-1" – yelled Katelyn. No one moved. Katelyn managed to retrieve her cell phone and made the call. Waiting for the ambulance to transport Pearl to the hospital, Andrew noticed his mother turning blue. David immediately started performing mouth to mouth resuscitation on his mother in law in an attempt to revive her. It wasn't long before the paramedics came and took over. On the way out the door, the Mayor whispered in one of the paramedic's ear. Looking at the Mayor as if he mis-heard him, the Mayor assured him he'd heard correctly. "Okay," was all the paramedic said, and then they left.

David rode in the ambulance with Pearl. On what should have been a very short ride, David realized they were going in a different direction. "Where are we going? He asked the paramedics.

"To Heritage Hospital over in Wilson." The paramedic responded nonchalantly.

"Why are we going over there when the hospital here is only minutes away. I am a doctor and this woman needs immediate care," shouted David.

"Don't care. We don't take coloreds in this town." The driver kept driving ignoring David's words.

It suddenly hit David. Everything Katelyn told him about Anna played like a movie in his mind. This town was really hung up on a rule that didn't make any sense. Especially in today's time. Refocusing his attention on Pearl, David assured her again she would be okay. They would be at the hospital soon. He wasn't sure if Pearl understood him, but he needed to say it more for himself than her.

Chapter 21

The Aftermath

The crowd standing in disbelief was motionless. No one was sure what to do next. Katelyn and Andrew stared at each other, numb. Sharon acted immediately by gathering their things and getting the family out of there. The children visibly shaken by what they just witnessed needed to be removed as quickly as possible. Grace was crying hysterically and needed consoling.

Once outside and safely in the limo, Katelyn wrapped her arms around Grace, stroked her hair and told her it was going to be okay. Grace continued to cry. The boys sat quietly. No one was sure what to say or do.

"We have to go to the hospital." Katelyn's voice was shaky but tried to remain calm for Grace.

"Wait a minute. Let's talk this out, Sharon said. There are many things to consider here. Do we want the children exposed to anything else tonight? Look at them. I don't think it's a good idea."

"What are you saying Sharon? We can't go see our mother?" Katelyn tilted her head to one side trying to understand Sharon's logic. *Yes, they were going to the hospital. It was their mother. Where else would they be?* Katelyn thought.

"We all just experienced something horrendous. I love Pearl as much as you and Andrew. But we have four children who are traumatized and need us as parents tonight. Besides David is with her, he will let us know her status. We can make a better decision then." Sharon looked at Andrew for his support.

"She's right, Andrew agreed. Let's focus on the children right now and wait for David to call."

Katelyn knew they were correct in their assessment. Grace was clinging to her for dear life. But Katelyn wanted her mother to know she was not alone. Desperately wanting to be with her. It wasn't a fight she could win, so she agreed.

Andrew instructed the driver to take them home. Without getting into much detail with the children, they tried to explain how there are some people who want to see other people suffer for no real reason. There were also mean-spirited people in the world and they had just witnessed one. Katelyn stayed with Grace until she fell asleep. Sharon and

Andrew stayed talking with the boys until they felt comforted. No one talked about the actual point Irene made in her so-called speech.

When the three adults felt it was safe to talk, they gathered in the study, closed the doors and looked at each other, confused. Katelyn wide eyed and exhausted at the same time asked, "What the hell did we just witness? I told mother Irene Pritchard could not be trusted."

"Why would she?" ......before Andrew could get the words out the phone rang. He reached for it quickly not wanting it to wake the children.

Clearing his throat, Andrew answered, "hello."

"Andrew it's David. I don't have much time to talk. Pearl has had a stroke. The doctor assigned to her case is suppose to be the best. She is sure it is an ischemic attack, meaning she should fully recover. Pearl is partially paralyzed which is unusual in these types of strokes, but the doctor is sure it is temporary."

"Is this good news David?" Andrew wasn't sure.

"Yes. It's really good news. She has a bit of a road ahead, but she is healthy otherwise and should make a full recovery."

"We plan to be there first thing in the morning." Andrew took it upon himself to make the decision.

"Well, Andrew that might not be such a good idea." David was hesitant in bringing up the matter.

"Why?" Andrew sounded concerned.

"If I were you, I would take as much stuff as you can and get out of Anna. Andrew… they wouldn't take Pearl to the hospital there. We're over in Wilson at Heritage Hospital. For everyone's safety, get out of that town. I have to go but will call you tomorrow. I'm staying here tonight. Let me speak with Katelyn before I hang up."

Andrew handed Katelyn the phone. He walked over and put his arm around his wife, stunned by what he just heard.

"Hi Babe," Katelyn said when her brother handed her the phone.

"Hi," said David sounding tense. I won't go over everything I told Andrew, he will give you the details. Pearl is going to be okay we believe. Get some rest and I will see you tomorrow. I love you and I believe every word you've said about Anna." With that he hung up.

Holding the phone still in her hand, Katelyn asked Andrew for details of their conversation. When Andrew told Katelyn and Sharon what David said, they all agreed, they had to get out of Anna.

Chapter 22

Irene & The Mayor

"**W**HAT – THE – HELL -JUST-HAPPENED-HERE?!" Mayor asked Irene as he pulled her from the stage and into a side room.

"Didn't you hear what I said? Yes, right here under our noses for all these years a Nigger woman has been living here, and you didn't even know it."

Pacing back and forth, hand cupped around his chin, and looking as if he'd seen a ghost, the Mayor continued. "Hell, you didn't know it either. How did this happen? How did you find out?" Waving his hand as if to dismiss the thought, he picked up his pacing. "Where is Ridley? Get him in here. We have to find a way to handle this mess and bring order back to this town."

"I haven't seen him. I'm not sure where he is," Irene said.

"Did you tell him about this?"

"No, I told no one," Irene promised him.

"Why didn't you come and tell me?" The Mayor stopped pacing a second, waiting for Irene to respond.

"I knew how much you liked Pearl, and I didn't want you changing the rules of our town for one person. I don't care how good a person she has appeared to be. The rules are the rules Mayor," her arrogance returning.

"Are you absolutely sure about this? I mean, could there be some mistake? I simply cannot believe this," hoping Irene was somehow mistaken.

"I have had the very best investigator on this. There is no denying she is a nig…" Standing smug in her position, Irene was not going to let the Mayor ridicule her.

"Stop saying that word. I don't care for it." His tone stern. "I don't think I have ever heard you use it so don't start now." The Mayor stood against a chair for support as he scolded her.

"I never felt the need to use it until now. *They've* known *their* place. But to have one live among us. Deceive us. Act as if she was one of us. It makes me sick to my stomach Mayor. The gall of that woman. You can't stand there and tell me you don't feel betrayed by all of this?" Irene was adamant in her stance.

"Now I get to see what I heard people talk about for years." Ignoring Irene's question.

"I never cared what people thought about me. Don't turn this on me Mayor. What are you going to do about this?" Irene remained persistent.

"I don't know. I need time to process this. You've had days. I really need to talk to Ridley and find out the best way to handle this," standing with his back to Irene wishing it would all go away.

"There is a roomful of people out there who are waiting for a response from you and all you can say is you don't know." Irene was now standing beside the Mayor.

"You created this monstrosity, why don't you go and clean it up?" His aggravation was building with her.

"I knew this would happen. That's why I didn't come to you in the first place. I always knew you had a soft spot for that woman. Do something Mayor, or I will have to question your love for *those* people." Irene's tone was rising. She wanted the Mayor to know how serious she was.

"Don't threaten me Irene. You may bully other people in this town, but that's not going to work with me! I need time, and I am not going to do something because you want me to. I agree the people out there need to be told something. I just don't know what it should be at this point." The Mayor went back to his pacing.

At that moment, there was a knock on the door. Irene opened it.

One of the Mayor's body guards stood there with Mayor Bradley from a neighboring town. Irene stepped aside to allow the Mayor to enter.

"What's going on Carter?" He asked with a disturbed look on his face.

Before either could answer, there was another knock. The guard brought several more mayors and dignitaries. The Mayor finally put a stop to the interruptions.

"Don't allow anyone else back here," he instructed the guard. "Can you please let the people know I will be making a statement soon." The guard nodded and left.

"I thought…" Irene started.

The Mayor held up his hand before she could get the words out. "Don't say anything else. You've said enough."

Each mayor or dignitary asked their questions, the Mayor tried to answer them without allowing Irene to offer any explanation. They soon came up with a temporary solution to calm the people, while working toward a permanent one.

The town folk were dumbfounded by Irene's speech and wanted answers. As they watched Pearl being carried out on a stretcher, they simply didn't know what to make of it. What started out as a beautiful evening, was now a nightmare on Elm Street. They were all unwilling participants. But why would Irene say something so horrible against Pearl. Everyone loved her. Pearl and Irene were best friends; had been for years. Could Irene be correct in her information? She'd been known to embellish stories in her career. Was she doing so now?

The chatter continued among the people. Wondering what was going to happen next. What should they do? Should they go home or wait.

Pearl's family had gathered their things and left when Pearl was taken out. Therefore, no one could ask them any questions. Besides, did they know? Were they as surprised as everyone else?

A couple of women were gossiping in a corner. "You know, that Katelyn was always drawn to *those* people, remember? said one woman.

"Yeah, I remember when she was caught with that negro boy when she was about seventeen. Almost got the boy killed," another woman added.

"Do you think because she knew about Pearl she thought it was okay?" asked the first woman.

"I don't know," replied the other woman, "but I'm sure she knew the rules." The ladies went back and forth in their conversation. Speculating. Inventing. Wondering.

With the interruption of everything, it was a while before they realized the Mayor and Irene were out of the room. The whispers were more like bees buzzing by now, and everyone wanted answers. Surely, the Mayor and Irene wouldn't leave without addressing the people first.

Unsure how much time passed, when one of the Mayor's body guards took the stage. He informed the crowd the Mayor would be making a statement soon. That made the people talk even more. Too dignified to cause a ruckus, they only talked among themselves, but they expected the Mayor to rectify the situation swiftly. After all, they had to preserve the heritage of Anna.

It wasn't long before the Mayor reappeared and took the stage. Waiting for everyone to take a seat it allowed the Mayor to gather himself to address the people.

"I'm sure you are as shocked as I am to learn this information tonight. I'm also sure you want answers. The fact of the matter is, we won't get them tonight. I have spoken with Irene, who has assured me what she shared tonight is true. That's all we know. I will be looking into this myself, and I promise each of you, upon my findings, the appropriate actions will be taken. The best I can tell you is to go home, get a good night's sleep and I will be in touch with you soon."

As the Mayor turned to leave the stage, questions were being hurled from the crowd.

"I will not answer anything tonight because I don't have enough information. If anyone knows where Ridley is, have him contact me immediately." The Mayor left the stage after that.

The Mayors agreed Irene shouldn't go home. It was time for them to work on damage control, and they didn't want her to add any more fuel to this raging fire. The Mayor arranged for her to be taken to a hotel. She was not allowed to take her cell phone and was strongly instructed not to contact anyone. As much as she wanted to object, Irene knew they were right. She hadn't thought about the consequences of her actions, she just wanted the information to be exposed. Now that it happened, the spotlight was on her. Where was her support? Where was Ridley? Irene knew he would be furious, but for him not to stick around, she was not happy about that. Is this how it would be when they got married? She would not allow such behavior from him. Irene wanted to call him to let him know where she'd be, but the guards would not allow it. Trying not to be agitated, as she did create this fiasco, she adhered to their rule.

Once the guards escorted Irene home to get a change of clothes, she settled in at the hotel. As a precautionary measure they removed the phones from her room. One guard would remain outside her door. Should Irene need anything she was to let him know.

Sitting in her aloneness, Irene began to reflect upon her actions. Not one to admit being wrong in any situation, Irene simply blamed Pearl. If Pearl had not lied about who she was,

116

none of this would have ever happened. "That's why you can't trust *those* people," she heard herself say out loud. As soon as she said it though, Irene knew Pearl was not like that. They *had* been good friends, and Pearl was the finest woman she'd known. But, the rules were the rules and no matter how much she liked Pearl, she needed to be dealt with.

Irene hadn't thought about Katelyn, Andrew, or their children, and how all this would affect them. Why did she always have to be the one to tell the story first? It made her a great journalist, but it isolated her from a lot of people. You would think she'd learn, but she'd never learned to control that instinct. So now because of it she was alone. No Pearl, and no Ridley. Where was he anyway? Was he so angry with her that he didn't try to hear her side at all?

She lay in the darkness. Unable to sleep and left with all those thoughts running through her head.

Chapter 23

The Visit

Pearl heard the door open. She thought the doctor forgot to tell her something. To her surprise it was old man Ridley. Confused, she wasn't sure why he was there, or how he knew where to find her. Without saying a word, he lightly squeezed her hand and she felt safe. Giving her a reassuring look, he took a seat in the dingy worn chair by her bed.

She'd teased Irene about old man Ridley for years, and now he was sitting at her bedside. He had a stellar reputation in Anna and supported her philanthropic efforts over the years. A handsome and distinguished man, who'd aged well, was there in her hospital room. Pearl didn't know why. Ridley didn't say anything at first. He just sat in the dingy chair and looked as if he was carrying a heavy burden.

Pearl didn't know if he had spoken to the doctor or nurses to know her situation. She assumed by his silence and the compassionate look on his face he had. Why was he here and not her family? Was there something else going on she didn't know. She couldn't handle anything else.

For several minutes, all you could hear were the sounds of the machines in the dark dingy room. The smell more prominent than before. Pearl didn't want to be there, so why would he choose to be? She would have to wait until he broke the silence. The wait wasn't long.

"I am incredibly sorry for what happened to you. I knew Irene was capable of some underhanded things, but never this……not to you of all people." Ridley sat with his head bowed.

He was quiet again as if trying to find the right words. Pearl sensed his struggle. Lying, watching Ridley, still in his tuxedo, bowtie undone and shirt collar open, the stress of the evening was now evident on his face. But it was more than that. His words disrupted her thoughts.

"I was going to marry her." He paused again, as if waiting for a response. "Yes, after all these years. Irene finally said yes. I swear to you, I didn't know she was up to any of this. I would never be a part of such cruelty. I am wondering how she came across the information to use against you. I know she loves you and your friendship means something to her. I cannot for the life of me understand what brought her to this. Yes, we all are aware of Anna's history, but does that matter after all these years, especially for someone you love?"

For a moment, Pearl felt as if he was talking beyond this present situation. Ridley was wrestling with something else. Pearl continued to listen.

"I don't think I ever knew what brought you to Anna. I am sure it doesn't matter now. Whatever the reason, it only benefitted the town and Doc Swanson. I miss him you know. He was a great man. I'm sure you do too. You have done a lot to change the face of this town and your race shouldn't play a part in any of it. If it's true. Although, I don't think even Irene would tear such an important evening apart for something that wasn't."

Yes, Pearl was sure he was struggling with something. He seemed to ramble aloud in his thoughts as if she wasn't in the room. Shifting himself in the chair and running his fingers through his thick wavy hair Ridley continued.

"We all have things we struggle with. Irene included. I didn't want to fall in love with her, you know. As a matter of fact, I fought it for years. The tough exterior of that woman made me want to end our arrangement many times. Then the soft, loving Irene would appear, and I was drawn back. Since we spent so many years playing this cat and mouse game, I felt it was time to stop, make it legal and public. I'm convinced everyone knew anyway. We all know Anna is not that big. I used to tell Irene we were not fooling anyone."

Pearl wasn't quite sure where he was going with this conversation. The last thing she wanted to hear was anything regarding Irene Pritchard. She in large was the reason she was lying in a dingy hospital room on the outskirts of her home. What was this man doing here? Pearl was starting to feel agitated.

Ridley kept talking.

"Struggles. Yes. We all have things we struggle with. Do you remember when I came to Anna? Probably not. It was about ten years after you arrived, I think. You were not the only one trying to make a better life, if I believe Irene's claim. I am here to say to you, you are not alone. I identify with you. You see I too am a man of color. I came to…" Before he could get the words out of his mouth, the sound of alarms going off stopped him mid-sentence. Within seconds, nurses and the doctor rushed in the room to attend to Pearl.

"Sir, I am going to have to ask you to leave," ordered the doctor.

Checking Pearl's vitals, the doctor immediately saw her blood pressure was extremely elevated, and her heart was racing.

Dr. Parker ordered the nurse to give her 5mg of Nicardipine while snatching the covers from the bottom of her bed and started massaging her feet.

"Mrs. Swanson, we have to get your pressure down. We don't want you to have another stroke. She continued the massage.

"Come on Mrs. Swanson, I need for you to take some deep breaths and think of something happy. What do you want to do when we get you out of here? What's your favorite vacation place? Who in your life makes you happy?" The doctor kept massaging her feet.

Within a few minutes, Pearl's pressure and heart rate began to slow down and Dr. Parker discontinued her effort.

"Good job Mrs. Swanson. Now let's see if we can keep you right in this place. Your numbers are coming down, and it is very important we keep them there. I'm not sure what caused this, but, it is critical for you to remain calm." Dr. Parker lowered the foot she was holding back to the bed.

Pearl liked Dr. Parker's bedside manner. She probably was a good person overall and shouldn't be working at this hospital. Pearl also wanted to tell Dr. Parker what she just heard. All the years she kept her secret, thinking she was the only one in Anna, to find out old man Ridley was carrying the same secret. Pearl needed to remain calm, she didn't want to have another episode. But, this was a firestorm brewing, and it wasn't about to go away any time soon.

Tucking her covers back in place, Dr. Parker sanitized her hands and stood by Pearl's bedside.

"I want to see you walk out of here, Mrs. Swanson. That can't happen if we keep having episodes like this. I know this is tough for you, but let's both get some rest and I will check back with you in a few hours. Your son-in-law is here. I will let him come in but only if you promise to remain calm."

Dr. Parker had Pearl squeeze her hand if she understood. Pearl responded, so the doctor gave instructions to the nurse and left.

When Dr. Parker stepped into the hallway, Old man Ridley was waiting for her. Pulling him to a safe place for them to talk and not be overheard, the doctor spoke. "I told you I would only let you in to see her if you didn't upset her. What did you say? Did you tell her? This was not the time for you to have true confessions. Do you know what this could do to you, as well as your career?"

"I felt I needed to be here after what Irene did to her. She didn't deserve this. People like us only wanted to have a chance at a decent life. We just happened to land in Anna to get it." Ridley sounded apologetic.

"I told you years ago, Irene Pritchard was trouble, but you insisted on seeing her and look at where it has landed you." The doctor was angry with Ridley.

"None of that matters now. I just want to make sure Pearl is going to be okay." Ridley was trying desperately to change the subject.

"Do you know if her children are coming?" Dr. Parker asked Ridley. "Her son-in-law is here, but I haven't seen anyone else."

"I don't know anything at this point. I left as soon as I could without it being obvious. I didn't know her son-in-law was here. Where is he?" Ridley wanted to know.

"I let him in the doctor's lounge to make some calls. I'm assuming it's to the family."

"How is Pearl? Is she going to be okay? I didn't mean to upset her. I just got to talking and it all came out." Ridley was concerned for Pearl's wellbeing. Irene had done enough damage. He didn't want to be responsible for any more.

"Well I can't let you go back in there. It is not good for her and you need rest yourself. Doctor's orders." And if things go the way I think they will, Mrs. Swanson will be just fine. Now, seriously I want you to get some rest, you look tired.

"It may be doctor's orders, but I'm still your dad." Ridley kissed the forehead of his daughter and left the hospital.

Chapter 24

The Mayor & Ridley

Ridley dreaded going back to Anna. It was a terrible thing Irene did to Pearl and he wasn't sure if he could forgive her. He was unsure of anything at this point. Trying to figure out the best way to handle it all, he'd arrived home before he realized it. He sat in his garage, sullen. Things had gone well for many years, and he had to take up with the one woman who could destroy them all. Ridley couldn't wrap his mind around how Irene could be vindictive enough to tear a town apart. The town she said she loved and to the woman who had been her friend for more than fifty years. It was all surreal. Sitting in his car, tie untied, and shirt unbuttoned, Ridley felt defeat for the first time in a very long time. Better yet, he knew the Mayor would be looking for him. He had to come up with a strategy to quiet the town folk. He already knew what would be said; he'd heard it before on numerous occasions about *those* people. He never responded. It was different now though; he would either turn his back on what was happening to Pearl or get out of Anna before he was discovered. He'd made his choice. He hadn't come up with the how, but as an attorney he knew a huge injustice was taking place and it was time to do something about it. People would be hurt and betrayed, but they already were, so to hear his truth made him empowered. Besides the laws had changed and what they could get away with in the earlier history of Anna, wasn't legal today. It hadn't stopped the town folk though from enforcing the Sundown rule. Ridley had remained silent. It had pained him for years to see people of color rushing out of Anna each day as not to be a victim of the town's backlash. Of course, the town folk were too dignified to do anything themselves, but they had people on speed dial to take care of such things if the need arose. People of color knew this rule and very rarely were there any incidents. *Why had he stayed?* thinking to himself. He wasn't sure, and it didn't matter right now.

The phone interrupted his thoughts. He'd turned it off when he went to see Pearl and must have inadvertently turned it back on. When Ridley picked up his phone there were 27 missed calls mainly from the Mayor and he was calling again now. Ridley didn't answer. He wanted to make calls before he talked to the Mayor. It was best until he could work out the solution for everyone. It had been a long day, and he was tired. What he wanted was a hot shower, a stiff drink, his warm bed, and a plan for the next day.

When the morning arrived, Ridley was awakened by the phone. He knew it was the Mayor. Once again, Ridley refused to answer. The Mayor would have to wait a bit longer. As he sat on the side of the bed Ridley reflected on his life and couldn't help but think about Pearl. A woman who like himself, just wanted a better life. Never bothered anyone, simply wanted to make a difference in the lives of people. When he started to win the trust of the town folk and grow his legal practice, he soon put the color of his skin in the back of his mind. By the time Ridley brushed his teeth and got ready for the dreaded day, he stood staring at the person in the mirror for a long time trying to find the man who'd come to Anna years back; but only seeing the person he'd allowed himself to become.

The call came he had been waiting for, and he headed to the Mayor's office. He dreaded each step. Not only was he fighting for himself and Pearl, he was fighting for every person of color who had and would pass through Anna. It was time for the injustice to end. No one had attempted this before, and now it was time. Past time.

"Where in the hell have you been?" The Mayor wasted no time when Ridley entered his office. "Better yet, why haven't you answered my calls?" Pacing back and forth as he had with Irene the night before, his anxiety was obvious. Not waiting for an answer, he proceeded with his questioning. "What do you know about this Pearl situation? The Mayor stopped pacing and looked at Ridley.

"I'm not sure I understand the question you are asking?" Ridley being cautious in his response.

"Oh, hell, stop acting like you and Irene haven't been sleeping together for years. Everyone knows it, and now is not the time for this game." He waved his hand as to dismiss Ridley's response. "What did Irene tell you about this?"

"Nothing. I had no idea about any of this," said Ridley.

"You mean to tell me that woman who can't keep anything kept this from you? I can't believe it. I just can't believe it." The Mayor was shocked.

Ridley sat watching the Mayor pace back and forth. His starched white shirt seemed to tighten around his neck.

"Irene has always been her own person. She has proven time and time again she will stop at nothing to prove a point." Ridley couldn't help but look disappointed by her actions.

"The question is my friend, how are we going to handle this situation?" The Mayor was matter of fact.

"Exactly which situation are you talking about Mayor?" Ridley still cautious in his response.

"Are you alright man? This Pearl situation. How do we handle it?" The Mayor's arms were flailing.

This was Ridley's moment of truth. Time for him to come clean. Time to work the law to his advantage.

"Legally, Mayor, there is nothing that can be done. Don't misunderstand me, I am fully aware of the rule here in Anna, but a rule is not a law. Besides, what are you going to do? Call up *the boys* and have them run her out of town. I don't think that would be smart right now. She's lying in a hospital not knowing if she is going to live or die. Would you really have them do more harm to her?" Ridley didn't want to sound as if he was pleading with the Mayor, but part of him was.

The Mayor looked at him as if a light bulb had gone off. "You never told me where you were last night after all this happened." He waited for Ridley to reply.

"I went to see her." Ridley never looked up at the Mayor. He sounded apologetic, but it wasn't his intent.

"You did what? What the hell made you do such a foolish thing?" The mayor now agitated, and it was reflective in his voice.

"There were some things I needed to know, and the only way to know was to go and see her." The lawyer voice took over.

"Well man, don't make me pull it out of you. What did she say? Did she give you answers to this bizarre story Irene is telling?" The Mayor didn't hide his anxiousness.

"She can't speak, so I don't have any answers." Ridley was looking directly at the Mayor now.

The Mayor started to speak but paused after he heard Ridley's words. The two men sat quietly, each contemplating what to say or do next.

"Pearl's a fine woman. One of the finest I've ever known." The Mayor spoke in a sympathetic tone. "But you know the people here will never let me give her a reprieve. Hell, they are hounding me now for answers."

"Mayor, it is time for this to cease. It has gone on too long. The times have changed. The only thing that hasn't is the people of this town. You cannot legally invoke a rule that isn't on the law books." Ridley was trying to appeal to his senses. "Besides you just said yourself Pearl is the finest person you know. Use that to prove your point to the people here. This is your time to show them it is not about the color of one's skin. *They* can't be good enough just to clean your house or cook your meals; it is more to *them* than that. Has anyone here ever tried to get to know a person of color beyond those things. They all are people at the end of the day. Why do you insist on treating them like second class citizens?" Ridley knew he was treading on thin ice with this conversation.

"Why are you so concerned about *those* people now? Is it because of Pearl or is it something else? Whose side are you on here? I need for you to back me on whatever I decide." The Mayor sounded desperate.

"I will not break the law for you or the people of this town Mayor. I will not be party to any injustices brought on to innocent people." The lawyer voice was back.

"We need to be united Ridley." The Mayor's agitation was becoming more evident. "What is wrong with you today? You seem different." The Mayor gave Ridley a serious look.

Now was the moment of truth. It was time to end it all. To come clean and reveal his secret. Ridley took a deep breath. He knew his life was about to be over in Anna, and he'd made peace with it. He took another deep breath.

"I *am* different. But not in the way you think. I went to see Pearl because I could relate to her plight." Ridley was slow in his speech.

The Mayor stared at Ridley for what seemed like eternity. His look was like trying to see something that was lost. In the Mayor's attempt to connect what he'd just heard, the color drained from his face. He stood frozen as he finally did. It was obvious he didn't know what to say. When he could find words, he would have to choose them wisely. He needed to sit. Making his way to his desk, the Mayor slumped in the mahogany leather chair.

"Has everyone in this damn town gone mad? What the hell do you mean *different* and you can *relate*?"

"You know what I'm saying, Mayor. Don't make me spell it out." Ridley got up to leave. He knew his time just ran out. He'd already made the necessary arrangements to leave. This was a loose end he needed to finish before he left.

The Mayor sat, stunned. Red-faced, not knowing whether to curse Ridley or kill him. How dare this man deceive him of all people. He'd always thought of Ridley as an honorable man. He would have given him everything he had if he needed it. How could he not have known? First Pearl, now him. How many others were there? How was he supposed to explain this to the people? If this got out it would be an uncontrollable mess. He had to maintain order, but he also could not let this matter go unnoticed.

"I don't expect you to understand nor am I looking for anything from you or this town. I know how you operate. I am making plans to depart Anna and will make sure I am out by Sundown. He turned to leave without looking back at the Mayor. Ridley's heart was heavy. This was one of the hardest things he'd done. He had tried cases that were much easier. He would have traded any of those cases to avoid this moment.

The Mayor was left seated in his office. Looking at the custom book shelves, the plaques on the wall, the many pictures he had taken over the years, his eyes landed on the whiskey decanter surrounded by two crystal glasses. He desperately needed a drink. Still in a daze, he poured himself a double, loosened his tie, sat back in his chair, picked up the phone and made the one call he knew he would regret.

Chapter 25

Irene & Ridley

When Ridley left the Mayor's office, he felt somewhat relieved. He'd not given much thought about his race in recent years; simply allowed himself to fit into the mold that was set in Anna. His sole purpose was to make a good living to provide for his daughter when his wife died and to find happiness in his life. He never knew it would be with Irene Pritchard, the nosey news anchor, and one of the most disliked people in town. He remembered meeting her during an interview after a lawsuit where the hospital had been sued for a wrongful death. They hit it off okay and soon would meet out of town when she was travelling for a story or late night at his or her place. She never wanted anyone to know about their *friendship*. She wanted to spread gossip, not be the subject of it. He'd honored her request in the early years as he was still building his credibility. But as the years passed and they both were getting older, it made him reconsider the nature of the relationship. Aging is something one never wants to do alone, and it was time to take this to another level. That was before Irene had to go and ruin it by exposing Pearl's secret. By doing so it had now placed him in an impossible situation with her and his status in Anna. Lost once again in his thoughts, he realized he'd been driving for half an hour on auto pilot with no destination in mind. Shaking his head to clear the distraction, he got his bearings and headed to see Irene. He'd at least managed to get that information from one of the Mayor's guards before the Mayor gave instructions regarding him. He knew the Mayor wouldn't be thinking about him going to see Irene, but on getting him out of town and all that came with it. Knowing he had a small window, he needed to move swiftly to see Irene.

When he arrived at the Hotel, he was sent right to her room. Good, he thought. He was correct thinking the Mayor had not thought about this yet. When he arrived at her room, a guard stood to greet him.

"Hello, Mr. Ridley."

"Hello, Barry. I'm here to see Irene."

"Sure." Without hesitation, he swiped his key card and let Ridley in.

When Ridley entered, Irene was finishing her lunch and was surprised to see him.

He spoke first.

"We have a lot to talk about, you know."

"Hello, to you too." Irene stared him down. She still thought he was the most handsome man she'd ever seen. Her pride would never let him know it though.

"I am serious Irene. I don't have a lot of time, and you and I need to have a serious conversation."

"Converse away. I have nothing but time since the Mayor has me in seclusion." Still the same smug Irene. Never wanting to take the blame for anything. She graciously moved her dishes to the other side of the table.

"It's for your own good after the stunt you pulled last night. What were you thinking? You and Pearl have been friends for fifty years."

Sitting there in her white satin blouse and navy slacks, he couldn't help but notice she was still a very beautiful woman. But that's where it stopped. She could be gentle, loving and kind, but her behavior in the last twenty-four hours had not displayed any of those traits.

"The stunt I pulled? I think you need to re-phrase that. Pearl is the one who pulled the stunt. No, you will not put this on me Ridley. She got what she deserved. Coming into our town befriending everyone, marrying Doc Swanson, raising those kids like they were her own. Even running this town socially, getting everyone to like her, while laughing behind our backs. No, she is the one who can't be trusted. I knew you couldn't trust *those people*. They just need to stay in their place and go back to their kind at the end of the day."

She squirmed in her chair as if she had just finished scolding him while making her point.

Ridley still standing, watched her gesture and couldn't believe he had fallen for such a person. Moving to sit in a chair across from her, he reluctantly sat.

"Do you realize what you've done? You have altered the life of a woman who has done nothing but good here in such a way that her life literally hangs in the balance. Take the race card out of it for just a moment Irene, and you must admit, she is still the same honorable woman she always was. The same woman fifty years ago, you decided to befriend. The same woman who changed the heartbeat of this town. You can't see past her ethnicity and for that you were willing to destroy her, her family and this town based on one divided rule." He leaned across the table as he spoke, to make sure he was delivering his point effectively.

"It doesn't matter." She waved her hand as she spoke. "Anna has prided itself on being prestigious without any crime or destruction brought by *those* people. I didn't make the rule, I am just upholding it because I like feeling safe here and not having to worry about being robbed or assaulted whenever I leave my house. I like the peace and tranquility that's here, and there is nothing wrong with me wanting to live this life. *They* are the intruders. *They* have their place and *they* need to stay in it."

Leaning back in his chair, Ridley couldn't believe his ears. This was imbedded deep within her. He thought he had made a difference with her, but now realized it was never going to change. His plan to take her with him wasn't going to happen. It was time for her moment of truth. It was hard to believe this woman who had traveled the world, received awards for outstanding journalism, was so narrow-minded in her way of thinking. He had to make her understand it wasn't about the color of one's skin. Yes, he had to make her see how wrong she was. He got up, poured himself a drink without saying a word. She awaited his response. He took a gulp from the glass and sitting it firmly on the table, he began to speak.

"It is unfortunate you feel that way. There are good and bad people in this world and race doesn't have anything to do with it. Bigotry is such an ignorant thing and *those people* you keep referring to, have more intelligence than Anna collectively. They have not allowed the shallowness of this town to hinder them from living their life even if it is outside of here. They don't live in a world divided. They choose not to, and it does come down to a choice."

Irene still sat with an arrogant disposition.

"What you fail to realize is you don't know everything, and you certainly don't control everything." The whiskey was starting to kick in, and Ridley was gaining more courage. He let out a smirk and shook his head.

"If you have something to say, Ridley, say it. Stop talking in all these riddles." Her aggravation with him was evident.

He smirked again. "I almost had you. You agreed to be my wife, but you had to go and ruin it all by exposing Pearl. You are a piece of work. But you know what Irene, what goes around comes around. You spent all that time exposing Pearl, who's going to expose you?"

"What are you talking about? I don't have anything to be exposed. Are you talking about us? Everybody has suspected something was going on with us for years, I just never acknowledged it. That's no big deal. I'm done with this. This conversation is over. I'm not going to sit here and listen to you ramble on about things that are insignificant to me. Pearl shouldn't have lied to us, and she got what she deserved."

As she rose to leave the table in an attempt to be in control of the conversation, Ridley hit the table with his hand. It startled her.

"Sit down Irene, I am not finished with you yet.

"I will not sit down. This conversation is not going anywhere, and I am done with it." She turned to go toward the bedroom.

"Let's see what the town has to say when they find out you've been sleeping with a black man all these years." He took the last of the drink.

Irene stopped dead in her tracks. She could not have heard him correctly. As if reading her mind, he assured her she had.

Irene turned back toward him. "What in the hell did you just say to me?" Her voice raised.

"You heard what I said the first time, Miss Irene Pritchard. You've spent so much time destroying Pearl for being a black woman while the entire time you were sleeping with a black man. Go figure."

Ridley got up to leave.

"Don't you dare walk out of here after saying that to me! Why are you trying to hurt me?" Irene couldn't believe Ridley was serious.

He kept walking. She picked up the glass from the table and threw it in an attempt to get his attention. The guard knocked and entered.

"Is everything all right in here? he asked.

"Everything is just fine," Ridley said to him. "Irene just dropped a glass."

The guard looked to get some reassurance from Irene. Agreeing with Ridley, the guard closed the door.

"How does it feel Irene? To know for once you don't have the upper hand, and you cannot control *this* situation. I am not saying any of this to hurt you. I loved you for a very long time, but after last night, I really don't know who you are. Maybe knowing this will give you something to think about. I am the same man you've been sleeping with all these years. Do you feel different about me now? Yes, I am a black man who came to Anna looking for a better life. I found it. I made a lot of friends here, and I've made a difference. Now that I have accomplished it, my time here is obviously up. Do with the information however you choose. Just know the Mayor is aware of it, so you can't act as if this conversation never took place."

He didn't wait for a response. For the first time in a very long time, Irene Pritchard was speechless. Ridley opened the door, said good-bye to the guard and left.

Irene could not believe what she just heard. How dare Ridley tell her such foolishness. She felt her cold heart beat loudly in her chest and knew what he said was true. Dropping to the floor she lay there, numb at the news. How would she survive this? The humiliation. The ridicule. The shame. Looking at the broken glass in front of her, she grabbed a piece, closed her eyes and slit her wrist.

Chapter 26

Reality

A heaviness fell over Ridley as he walked through the lobby of the hotel and out to his car. His life in Anna was rapidly coming to a close. It was bittersweet. He'd never thought it would end this way. But here he was. He had to see this through to the end. It would be a long drive to his house, and what would be waiting for him when he arrived made it even longer.

Ridley couldn't help but pause before turning the ignition. He knew the Mayor made *the* phone call when he left his office. Anything could happen to him now. But Ridley also knew the Mayor well enough to know nothing would appear too obvious. No, whatever the Mayor ordered would look like an accident in some way, and Ridley had an idea of what it would be. He was so sure he'd stake his legal reputation on it. Looking at the time on the dashboard, he knew he didn't have much time to get out of Anna.

When he pulled into his neighborhood, he parked a street over and waited. The mature trees perfectly spaced and the privacy fences surrounding the beautiful homes kept the ugliness from the outside world. These same things would keep him from being noticed in the interim, but not for long. If Ridley planned the Mayor's move correctly, what he dreaded most was about to take place. The door opened from the passenger's side, which startled him. Sharon slid in the seat. Ridley needed to be more careful as he didn't see or hear her approach.

"Where did you park? Did you do as I instructed?" Ridley asked obviously concerned.

Sharon assured him great care had been taken. The taxi let her out a street over and she'd walked over undetected.

"This is not my first rodeo, you know. I've chased a few stories in my day."

Ridley hardly recognized her, dressed in all black and sporting a baseball cap. Sharon looked completely different from the perfectly polished anchor who covered the evening news.

"Well, if we get this right, you may just get to add another trophy to your collection for outstanding journalism," Ridley said nervously.

"This is a very interesting story and certainly news worthy. I've heard Andrew and Katelyn talk about this stuff, but always felt parts of it was embellished. When you called and confirmed most of what they'd been saying was true, I had to be a part."

Sharon unzipped the black bag on the floor between her feet pulling her camera equipment and other essentials from it. Wrapping the strap around her neck she attached the camera to it. Flipping her baseball cap backwards, Sharon looked through the lens to make the needed adjustments. Not wanting to miss anything, she was prepared to capture the impending show. She felt bad for Ridley. She could only imagine how hard this must be for him. But if he must leave his home, exposing the town should bring him relief from a forced exit. The world was changing, and it was time for Anna to change also.

It was just about dusk when they heard doors slam on Ridley's street. The two looked at each other and they knew it was time. Sharon immediately opened the door and made her way across the road to the back of the fence that surrounded Ridley's house. Ridley, however, hadn't moved so quickly. Sharon had more youthfulness on her side. He soon followed warning her to be careful. It could be dangerous for them both.

"Stop talking," she'd warned, and tipped to the side of the fence. Sharon could hear men talking but couldn't make out exactly what they were saying. Something about let's make this quick. She heard two sets of footsteps go to one side of the house and two sets on the other. She and Ridley exchanged a quick glance and waited for what was about to happen next. The wait wasn't long. The sound of liquid pouring, and the smell of gasoline made them move quickly. Easing by the side of the fence they moved to the opposite side of the street. With her camera in complete video mode, Sharon began filming. She started by capturing the trucks and license plates. With full view across the street, she didn't miss one thing. Within seconds, the flames erupted from the back of the house, the men rushed to their trucks, while Sharon captured it all on video. In their haste to leave they hadn't noticed Sharon or Ridley across the street. Ridley, his heart racing and feeling weak leaned against an old oak tree to steady himself. The house which had been home was now in flames. Making sure Sharon had the footage she needed, they cut through the neighbors on the opposite side of the burning house and made their way back to Ridley's car. Once safely inside, Ridley closed his eyes, took a deep breath, and with trembling hands, dialed 9-1-1. Seeing how shaken he was, Sharon offered to drive.

"We need to get out of here before the neighbors see what's going on and the fire department comes." Sharon knew the danger of them being seen. Ridley didn't argue with her. Staggering in his first couple steps when he got out to walk to the other side of the car, Sharon realized just how shaken he was.

Driving out of the neighborhood, they took the back entrance, careful not to be seen. Adrenaline rushing through their veins, they were both grateful Ridley suspected something of this nature may take place. Having worked with the Mayor and the people of Anna, Ridley knew his news would not bode well. And he was right. Wringing his hands together to steady his nerves, taking deep breaths to calm his irregular heartbeat, he closed his eyes again. The first part of his plan worked, now on to the second part of it.

Sharon drove fast but not enough to make anyone suspicious. She wanted to be long gone from Anna before the news of the fire spread among its residents. Besides, she needed to get the footage she'd just captured uploaded to her TV station for the late-night news.

"Are you okay?" She asked. Making sure Ridley was not more affected by the fire than he was letting on. Sharon could hear him taking deep breaths. As an older man the last thing they needed was a medical emergency right now.

"Yes, I am okay. A bit shaken, but I will be okay. I heard of such things you know, but to see it firsthand…it's surreal. I lived among these people. Hell even got some of them out of legal trouble over the years. Was I fooling myself to believe it would never happen to me? Maybe, just like Pearl, I thought I could make a difference." Ridley sounded sad and disappointed.

"You have made a difference. Both of you. And it has nothing to do with the color of your skin, it has everything to do with character and hard work. I don't believe either of you have taken anything from anyone. You have given more than any other human beings I know, and I know a lot of people. This has been a long time coming for Anna. If this town wasn't exposed now, then when? You are the only person who could do this. I know you didn't want it to happen this way, but the town left you no choice. And tonight and no later than noon tomorrow, the world will know about the inner workings of Anna." Sharon believed every word she said to Ridley.

"Thank you for doing this. I know you and your family are dealing with so much regarding Pearl. I couldn't do this without you. I will never forget it or be able to repay you." Sincerity exuded from Ridley.

"Telling the story and exposing this town is the only payment or thanks I need. Pearl is dear to all of us and the last couple of days have been tough especially with the children. We have been forced to have conversations with them on a level none of us expected." Sharon went on to explain how the night of the dinner had affected them all.

They continued to talk about the rest of their plan. Every now and again Sharon checked the mirrors to make sure no one was following them. It wasn't long before they'd arrived at their destination. They both breathed a sigh of relief.

Chapter 27

The Beginning of the End

Katelyn and Andrew had been working on setting everything in motion for Sharon and Ridley to arrive at Pearl's new home. This night would change Anna forever. Katelyn felt relief from the anger she'd carried toward Anna for many years.

The last couple of days they'd pushed plans ahead to remove Pearl's things from Anna. Knowing everyone was still reeling from the news. The distraction was what they needed. Neighbors stood on their lawns to watch the movers collect things from the beautiful manor they'd spent years enjoying. None would dare lower themselves to lend a hand or offer support. They were too dignified for that. They were waiting to see what the Mayor had to say about all of this. After all it was his job to keep order in the town.

Katelyn and Andrew exhausted from the events of the last two days had to be a part of Ridley's plan when he called. The two spent the last couple of hours putting together a make-shift studio for Sharon. Her interview with Ridley along with the footage was going to be monumental. Glad to be out of Anna, made it easier to accomplish this undertaking.

It wasn't much longer before the doorbell rang. They knew it was Sharon and Ridley. Andrew answered the door and embraced his wife, grateful she was okay. He shook Ridley's hand and invited him in, asking him to excuse the mess. The *mess* as he referred to, were boxes to be unpacked. A task that would have to wait as they had more important matters to attend.

The four sat at the dining room table, one of the rooms that had been somewhat set up. Sharon and Ridley recapped what they'd witnessed, each feeding off the other's recount. Sharon excused herself to upload the footage to the station. The interview with Ridley would be live as the footage played in the background. She planned to end the interview with Andrew and Katelyn speaking about their mother.

Andrew showed Ridley to a bedroom on the lower floor to shower and prepare for the interview. He retrieved the suitcase Ridley managed to pack from the trunk of his car. As he gathered the piece of luggage, he saw boxes of mementos and other keepsakes. His heart sank at the realization of how this was bigger than all of them. Returning to the house he put the suitcase on the bed, knocked on the bathroom door to let Ridley know and quietly left the room.

Walking down the hallway Andrew thought about his mother. Desperately wanting to see her, hold her and tell her how much he loved her. He thought about how he wouldn't be who he was today if Pearl hadn't been a part of his life. Jon interrupted his thoughts when he entered the family room by asking about something in a box. The teenagers were phenomenal in helping to get Pearl's things in order. They understood the importance for them to move forward. Jon took control over keeping his brother and cousins busy by assigning them tasks. It allowed the adults to handle the issue at hand without constantly having to answer questions. For the most part it worked well. Occasionally, Jon would get a question he would answer to the best of his ability, but when he couldn't he would say something like "adults are complicated, who can understand them." It was enough to get them back on track, until the next question arose. His plan was working, and they'd accomplished much in a short period of time.

Jon knew when his Mother was interviewing Mr. Ridley, to keep the others upstairs. He was willing to do whatever was necessary to help bring his grandmother home.

Sharon showered, dressed, and headed downstairs to refine her notes. Ridley was coming down the hall to join her.

"You clean up well," she complimented him.

"Thank you. You don't do so bad yourself," Ridley returned the compliment.

The two chuckled. It was the first time since this all started anyone said anything remotely humorous.

Katelyn and Andrew joined them. They discussed the strategy for the interview. After they all agreed, Sharon checked her email to make sure they were ready to get started, confirmed the air time with the station, and the second part of the plan was put in motion.

The tripod she'd rented earlier stood perfectly positioned behind the camel colored leather sofa in the family room. The lighting wasn't quite the way she would have preferred, but it would have to make do. They were in a pinch; besides, the story was more important. Sharon began to feel the magnitude of the situation. Closing her eyes, she inhaled. Ridley noticing the gesture, became concerned.

"Are you sure you want to do this? I know I've asked a lot of you today. You can back out now if this is too much, it is my story and my responsibility." Ridley was sincere in his inquiry.

Before she could answer, Katelyn chimed in sounding desperate in her response. "We have to. Mother's life literally depends on this story being told."

"I agree," Andrew rising from his chair went and knelt beside his wife, "but if this is too much for you Sharon we can end this right now."

"No, I am fine," shaking her head. "It's been a long day. I guess it's catching up with me." Repositioning herself in the Bergére chair that complemented the sofa, she was ready to begin the interview.

When the time came, Sharon told the story of Anna and its history. Hearing it told from someone other than themselves was all too surreal for each of them. Interviewing Ridley then Katelyn and Andrew, Sharon gained inner strength to get through the ugliness of the story. It was especially hard to see the footage from the fire. She ended the interview by sending a special message for Pearl to hang in there, and they would see her soon. When it was over, they took a deep breath and knew their lives would never be the same. Andrew left the room; the other three being unsure why, reemerged with four glasses and a bottle of wine. It was all they had in the house. He knew they could all use a drink. Sitting in the quiet, no one sure what to say, Jon interrupted the quietness.

"Is it okay for us to come and eat now?" His voice sounding apologetic.

Andrew stood to acknowledge him, walked over and put an arm around his shoulder. At six feet Jon was as tall as his father.

"Thanks for handling things upstairs while we did this. It has been tough for us. I appreciate it. How are they?" Nodding toward the stairs, Andrew waited for Jon to respond.

"They've been great until a few minutes ago. We are concerned about Gramma and what this has done to our family, but they are good."

"Call them down, and we will find something for you guys to eat."

Patting Jon on the back, Andrew knew it was going to be harder than he'd made it sound. With everything happening so quickly over the last few days, they'd been living on fast food. Even the children were starting to complain. Andrew managed to food shop but on a limited basis. He wasn't sure if what he bought would suffice.

It wasn't long before the rustling of four teens bounced down the stairs. The sound broke the concentration of the others in the family room, and they prepared themselves for the children's engagement. They went straight to the kitchen bypassing the adults. The adults were relieved. They couldn't deal with questions at that point; still needing time to come down from the adrenaline high they'd encountered. Two people who had influenced Anna in such a tremendous way, now were doing so in a different one. When the segment aired, there would be no turning back, only moving forward.

When Katelyn looked over at Ridley, she could see the effects of it all on his face. The confident, bold, and highly intelligent man diminished to fleeing for his life because of injustice in a town. The ignorance shook her to her core. Katelyn never understood it as a child and even less as an adult. She had nothing but respect for Ridley and hoped whatever his next steps were for his life would be peaceful ones. She'd wondered what happened with Irene but wouldn't dare ask such a question now. It would come out eventually. Katelyn was pretty sure she was somewhere gloating on how she unraveled another story and destroyed someone's life. Having warned her mother for years about Irene, Pearl still chose to trust her. Pearl knew how Irene was, but never thought she would ever do anything like that to her. Their friendship ran too deep. In the end everyone knew Irene would sell her soul for a story. Anybody's story, and now they knew Pearl wasn't any different. Coming out of her thoughts, Katelyn looked at Ridley again and suggested he lie down in the bedroom he used earlier to shower. He didn't refuse the offer. The day brought too much activity and he was exhausted. Ridley wasn't sure if he would sleep, but he wanted to at least rest.

###

In the kitchen, Andrew allowed the children to help with dinner. Although it was a Hodge podge of food, they were content to have something to eat. Trying to prolong the questions Andrew knew were coming, he instead asked questions pertaining to their assignments and what was accomplished. Each one gave their version of how things went, but all agreed Jon gave the orders but didn't feel he'd done much work. Andrew looked at his son and gave him a wink.

"That's what you do when you're in charge. It's called delegating. Apparently, he did it well."

The sly grin he was known for and always managed to charm Pearl with, seemed to have the same effect on the kids. After setting the table with paper plates and plastic ware, Andrew went to get the adults for dinner. When they'd sat at the table minus Ridley, the women looked at the prepared food. Trying hard not to show the "*what the hell is this*" look on their faces, the women were shocked at what they saw. Pasta, tuna, chips, and sliced fruit were all beautifully arranged on the table. Katelyn and Sharon looked at each other. Katelyn spoke first. "Hey guys, do you think you can wait about 30 minutes before we eat? This looks great, but I think I can make it a little better." She got disapproving looks.

"You can eat the fruit and the chips while you wait," Sharon said. There wasn't any objections. Katelyn grabbed the tuna and Sharon the pasta and headed for the kitchen. Katelyn found a casserole dish, mixed the tuna and pasta together, added mayo, milk and cheese to the mixture and slid it in the oven. Sharon made a salad with tomatoes and used seasonings and olive oil to make a dressing. They at least had those from the things packed from the move. It wasn't long before they were back at the table. The wait was well worth it. In a very short period of time, the make shift casserole and the salad were gone. Andrew looked at Katelyn and his wife and said a soft "thank you" to them both. It had been a long couple of days for them all. Running on autopilot was their new norm and they were just trying to make it all work.

Grateful the children were somewhat understanding, they'd gotten through another crisis, that of having a decent meal to eat. Thinking they were home free from questions, Grace asked about Pearl, and what was going to happen next. It was a question they all wanted the answer to. Before anyone could answer, the doorbell rang. It was David.

Chapter 28

The End?

The next morning the entire house woke to phones ringing. Each phone rang in melodic harmony. With one eye open Sharon looked at her phone to see it was the studio. She sat up, answered the phone with one hand and ran her other hand through her tousled hair. "Hello," she answered still half asleep.

"Can I tell you every major network has picked up this story?" Preston Lockhart, her station manager was shouting on the other end of the phone.

It took a moment for the news to sink in. Not waiting for her to respond, he continued. "I wasn't sure when you first told me about this story, if anyone would be interested, but the emails and phone calls we have received have been through the roof! I want you to do a continuation of this story before every major network contacts you for an exclusive."

Talking faster than she'd ever heard Preston speak in her entire career, Sharon was trying to follow the conversation. She heard him but wasn't quite comprehending.

"Wait Preston, I hear you and normally, I would be all into pursuing a story like this, but you have to understand this is my family. This story affects me personally. I need time to talk to them and see what works best for us in this situation. This is not business as usual. We have children to consider and my mother-in-law. I will get back to you on this. Give me some time please?" Sharon pleaded.

"No! What you don't understand is Anna is about to be flooded with reporters, camera crews and people coming to protest. You don't have time to think about this." Preston paused as if to consider his last words. He wasn't trying to be unsympathetic, but he had a business to run. Since they broke the story, it was only fitting for them to continue with the lead, especially since it did affect one of them.

Rising from the bed feeling fully awake, Sharon realized she was alone. She wasn't even sure what time it was. Hoping Andrew heard the conversation and would give her a nod or something for direction. But he wasn't there. Sharon's heart was now rapidly pulsating. The reporter in her wanted to jump right in, but the wife, mother, daughter-in-law and sister-in-law couldn't help but pause and protect her family. Looking around the room at boxes still needing to be unpacked and clothes strewn from their suitcases, the view was just as disheveled as her current situation. "I'll have to call you back Preston." And before Preston could respond, Sharon hung up.

Heading downstairs, Sharon heard Katelyn on the phone, Jon on his phone, Andrew on his, and Ridley coming up the hallway on his. She stopped before her feet reached the last step. Her phone rang again. It of course was Preston calling back. Sharon ignored the call, but realized she had seventeen missed calls. Had she slept so hard the night before that she didn't hear the phone? It was real and happening as fast as Preston said. She needed to let everyone know what they were in for, and she needed to do it now.

Sharon went to Andrew first. He was finishing a call from the hospital. Pearl had a restful night and her numbers were looking a lot better. There was movement in her hands and feet. The doctor was very hopeful. Upon ending the call, he saw the concern on his wife's face. "What's wrong?"

"We all need to talk, now." Her phone was still ringing. Sharon turned it off.

Entering the family room with Andrew behind her, Sharon waited for Katelyn to get off the phone. It was one of her neighbors calling about reporters all over their lawn and how they should handle it. Having seen the news, they wanted to ask questions, but didn't. Genuinely concerned, they just wanted to help. Katelyn assured them everyone was fine, thanked them for their concern and willingness to handle the reporters. Katelyn could see Sharon and her brother sitting anxiously across from her waiting for her to end the call. "What?" she asked cautiously placing her phone on the table.

Let's wait for Ridley as this is going to affect all of us," Sharon said pacing the floor.

"Okay, while we are waiting, let me make sure Jon is alright." Andrew left to find him.

Katelyn looked at Sharon with a confused look on her face.

"It's Avery. She and her family saw the news and wanted to make sure Jon and the rest of the family was okay." Sharon stopped her pacing and took a seat.

"I'm afraid this is the beginning and not the end," Sharon leaning in almost whispering to Katelyn. "That's what I need to talk to everyone about. We have decisions to make and I mean right now. We can't put it off."

"What are you saying?" asked Andrew as he re-entered the room.

"Listen, my station has informed me that every major news outlet has picked up this story and most of them are headed to Anna as we speak, and protesters are coming as well. Preston wants me to continue coverage of this story but I told him I couldn't and wouldn't until I spoke to you first. This affects us all." Sharon looked at Katelyn, Ridley and then Andrew.

Ridley picked up where she left off. "Let's start with the good things first. We are out of Anna, so they won't find us right away at least, and Pearl is not in the hospital in Anna, so that's also a plus. Sure, they will probably bombard Anna and it's to be expected, let's face it, who would think this kind of racism still existed today. It is news worthy, which is why it needed to be reported, but we must stay ahead of it and not let it control us. The concern right now is how to move forward. I suggest we take advantage of the fact they don't know where we are and work on a strategy to get through this."

"I agree with Ridley." They all looked at Andrew. As if he hadn't seen their reactions, he kept talking. "Let's focus on the here and now. This house still needs unpacking and the children need attention. Let's start there. It will give us a chance to think. We can come together later and talk about what to do next. Until then, everything else is on hold." His last sentence came across as a matter of fact, and it was received as such. The conversation shifted from Anna and its peril to tending to the matters at hand. Reluctantly, the women agreed. They called in the children, shared the game plan with a promise to do something fun later in the day and they all got to work.

By lunchtime everyone was ready for a break. Andrew went to the store earlier that morning when Sharon's phone kept ringing and interrupted his sleep. She hadn't moved. So, to make better use of his time, he and David who hadn't slept much either made the trip. Not wanting to repeat the food situation from the night before, Andrew thought it best to actually food shop. He was glad he'd thought about quick and convenient, but also sort of healthy foods to eat, knowing they still had much work ahead of them. David gave him more details about Pearl. He was confident she would be fine. Andrew let David know how appreciative he was for staying at the hospital with his mother.

"She's family, where else would I be?" asked David. The two men strolled each aisle trying to make the best food choices. When the shopping was over they headed home. The men talked very little on the drive back. Was it the weight of their situation that determined the silence, or the uncertainty of what to say or do next?

###

The assorted tray of wraps the men selected for lunch was an excellent choice. No one complained, and Andrew wasn't sure if it was because everyone was hungry, tired or both.

The men took the teens out for fresh air after lunch. It was agreed they needed a change of scenery. Ridley thought it best if Katelyn and Sharon remained home. They didn't want to take the chance of Sharon being recognized. When the men ventured out with the children, Katelyn and Sharon sat across from each other. The house was quiet for the first time since their arrival. Sharon leaned her head back on the sofa and closed her eyes. Unable to hold it any longer Katelyn let out a loud wail.

Chapter 29

True Confession

Sharon sat up startled by Katelyn's outcry. Not sure how to comfort her sister-in-law or the reason behind it, she immediately went to Katelyn's side.

Katelyn leaned into her sister-in-law and cried harder. Sharon could feel the vibration of Katelyn's pain. So, she held her sister-in-law while she cried it out. When everything she'd been holding for the last few days and possibly years were out, Katelyn pulled away from her.

"I'll be right back," Sharon said to her as she went down the hall to wet a washcloth. Sharon understood how stressful it had been for them but didn't realize the effect it had on Katelyn. Returning to the den, she handed Katelyn the cloth.

"Do you want to talk about it?" She asked her still visibly shaken sister-in-law.

Heaving from her outburst, Katelyn shook her head, no. She wanted to but couldn't form the words. She wasn't even sure the reason for the outburst, so she would have a hard time trying to get Sharon to understand it. Katelyn's heart ached, her spirit broken. Her anger fueled toward Anna for placing them in such an impossible position. Where would she start the conversation? The list was long, and she wasn't sure if Sharon would understand.

"You know we can talk about anything." Sharon pulled Katelyn's hair back to see her face.

"I...know." Katelyn struggled to get out the words. Holding the cool washcloth over her inflamed eyes, she began to take slow deep breaths to regain control of her breathing.

Sharon wanted to know the answer to the one question no one had addressed. This was the perfect time to ask it. She also knew it was part of what was bothering Katelyn.

"Katelyn, I want to ask you a question," Sharon said cautiously. "You don't have to answer it if you don't want to. I've wanted to ask Andrew for days now but didn't have the nerve."

"Yes." Katelyn answered without removing the cloth from her face.

Sharon wasn't sure if Katelyn was saying yes, she could ask the question or yes for the answer. She paused waiting for some direction. When she didn't get it, she asked the question for clarity. "Did you know Pearl was black?"

This time Katelyn removed the cloth and looked at her sister-in-law through swollen eyes. "Yes. Is it a problem?" Katelyn sounding almost confrontational.

"You know me better than that." Sharon was trying not to sound defensive.

"I take it you and Andrew have never talked about this?" Katelyn's voice was raspy.

"No. Never," was all Sharon managed to say.

"I am not surprised. There really isn't anything to talk about. She is the only mother we've known. Our mother died when we were both young. Our father raised us on his own with the help of nannies. He met my mother, dated for a few months and they were married. She was….is, our mother. We of course never knew to question anything. We were a family and we were happy. She nurtured us, loved us and that was all that mattered to us. She has always been special. Always saw the world differently than the other women here." Katelyn paused and drank from a bottle of water she'd brought earlier from the kitchen.

"When did you find out?" Sharon was intrigued with the story and positioned herself in a more comfortable spot on the sofa.

"When our father died, he left letters telling us about our mother. He wanted us to know in case anything like this ever happened. He didn't want us to be blindsided. It never mattered to either one of us and we never talked about it with her."

"How do you think your father knew?" Not wanting to sound like a reporter, Sharon was genuinely curious.

"I'm sure knowing Mother, she told him, and then again, he was a doctor maybe he just figured it out. It never mattered to him and it certainly didn't matter to us." Katelyn wiped her face again with the cloth.

"I know you never cared for Irene, but how do you think she found out about Pearl?" Again, not wanting to sound like a reporter, Sharon couldn't help but wonder about Irene's antics.

"That woman has destroyed so many lives with her meddling self. You're right, I never cared for her, even as a child. I warned mother time after time about trusting her, but she dismissed my concerns. So, to answer your question, I really don't know." Katelyn was trying hard to control her emotions.

Sharon was gaining more insight into the family dynamics. It was very interesting to her. They never talked about Pearl's past, so she never thought about it. Pearl was a great mother-in-law and a wonderful grandmother, so she hadn't concerned herself with unspoken things.

"Did Andrew tell you about the time I became *a bit too friendly* with a guy of *color* from another school?" Katelyn smirked.

"No, he didn't." Sharon didn't say much wanting to hear more about the encounter.

"Yes, we would see each other when we debated at different schools and became friends. He was really a nice guy. Greyson Fowler." Katelyn stared across the room as if Greyson was going to appear. "There was nothing between the two of us but friendship." There were some parents from here who traveled to the debates. They wasted no time telling my mother she needed to stop me from being so friendly with *that* person. 'You don't want her to have *a tainted* reputation,' they would say to mother.

"No!" Sharon gasped. "You can't be serious?"

"I'm very serious," Katelyn said with an almost embarrassing grin.

"Well, what happened?" Sharon was eager to hear the rest of this crazy story.

"Mother allowed me to talk to him on the phone, but I had to limit my interaction with him in public. She didn't want me to encounter any trouble from these narrow-minded people. I couldn't wait to get away from here. When I left for college I never wanted to come back. I only did because of Mother and Dad." Katelyn took a deep breath.

Sitting in absolute shock, Sharon didn't know what to say. She'd heard Katelyn and Andrew talk about Anna but was sure they were over exaggerating their stories. Apparently, they hadn't. "Did you keep in touch with him after high school?"

"Better than that, we dated the first two years of college." Katelyn smiled, reflecting briefly on those years.

"No way!" screamed Sharon.

"Yep, I sure did. One of the best men I've ever known. We are still friends to this day." Katelyn's red face was now beaming from delight.

"What happened. Why only two years?" Sharon was sitting straight up on the edge of the sofa hugging a pillow to control her emotions.

"It was me. I was in a dark place. Trying to find myself and figure out what I wanted to do with my life. Anna really messed me up for a while. I think part of my being with him was to prove I couldn't be controlled. I realized that wasn't fair to him, so I broke it off. He wasn't happy about it but understood, and we remained friends."

"Is that why you are so supportive of Jon and Avery?" asked Sharon. It never was an issue for Andrew or her.

"I sure am. We are in the 21st century. Anna is the only place still in the dark ages. Interracial dating is not even a topic of conversation nowadays. I want my nephew to have options and explore them. Not to be limited because the adults can't get it together. Besides, from what I hear Avery is smart and very pretty. I can't wait to meet her."

"I agree she is very pretty. Thank you for sharing that story with me. I promise I won't repeat it. I know how you feel about reporters, but I am *not* Irene Pritchard and you have nothing to worry about with me." Sharon wanted Katelyn to know she would never betray her trust.

"That's one thing I know for sure, you are not Irene Pritchard!" Katelyn let out a huge laugh.

Sharon joined in the laughter. She was glad to see Katelyn laughing. Sharon knew Katelyn had scars, but now understood why. There were other stories she was sure but would have to wait for Katelyn to share them in her own time.

After hugging each other, the women heard the chimes of the old grandfather clock in the foyer and realized how much time had passed. The men and teens would be back soon and would be ready for dinner. Katelyn ran upstairs to wash her face and look for eye drops. She didn't want them to see she'd been crying.

When they returned, the women had gotten over their earlier episode and were preparing dinner. The two women never spoke about that conversation again. Sharon had a new-found respect for her sister-in-law and understood fully why she was adamant on certain issues. She had good reason to be.

Pearl

Sharon was glad to be a part of this beautiful family. Having this insight should help tell the story the correct way.

Chapter 30

Anna's Demise

The Mayor couldn't believe how quickly news reporters and protesters invaded Anna. As if the town wasn't dealing with its own internal issues, this was way more than he'd expected. Normally, he'd have Ridley to help him through such an anomaly, but he had to go and screw things up. The town had gone to hell in a handbasket and he'd lost control. The people were angrier as each day passed. They wanted answers he didn't have to give. All because one woman was jealous of another woman, and the whole town was paying for it. Sitting in his chair, the Mayor looked out the window at what was once a perfectly quiet and peaceful town. It was being tainted by outsiders now. He knew legally there wasn't a leg to stand on. Ridley had been right about that. The Mayor reminisced on the times he tried to abolish the Sundown rule, but the town's elite would not stand for it.

They wanted to maintain the standard Anna had early on and were not open to any changes. So it remained. Deep down the Mayor knew it was wrong, but what was he to do when the entire town stood against any changes. He'd caved under the circumstances, allowed the money and power Anna held to dictate his actions. Two of the finest people he'd ever known were now being ostracized as a result of it all. Mainly by his hands who gave the order to torch Ridley's house. It was what the townspeople would have expected him to do, and he'd obliged it. The Mayor reasoned with himself on Pearl though. His split decision sent her to the hospital over in the "Bottoms." The Bottoms was a place outside of Anna known for its impoverished residents. Most of the residents worked in Anna as domestics. The term was used as a way of degrading people of color even more by reminding them of their sub-par socio-economic status. Pearl didn't deserve to be there, although no one really did, the Mayor kept telling himself. Once again, he would have encountered the backlash from the town, so he made the decision. As soon as he did, he regretted it. Still staring out the window yet looking at no one in particular the Mayor continued in his thoughts. *This is one hell of a mess.*

The only thing the police department, which was scarce consisting of ten officers, could do was keep peace. Crime was something Anna never worried about since it was full of elitists. Tapping his pen on the desk, the Mayor continued in his thoughts. *How dare Irene try to get out of this by slitting her wrists. Huh! She wasn't so strong after all. Just like a bully. Prey on the weak until the tables are turned on them. I'm glad she is going to be alright, so she can face every person she's ever tried to destroy.*

Turning his back to the forming crowd outside his window, the Mayor stood to start his routine of pacing back and forth. With his hands in his pocket and his head bowed, the pacing allowed him to figure out his next move. It didn't work. This was entirely too much for him. *The news. We have ended up on the damn news. Why the hell couldn't we be left alone.* The more he thought about Irene, the more he wanted to go to the hospital and strangle her.

A knock on the door interrupted his thoughts. "Not now!" he yelled.

The knocking continued.

"Didn't I say not now!" This time his voice vibrated through his office.

The knock was persistent. Agitated, he answered by snatching the door open. Before he could form the words to dismiss the person, there stood Randolph Billingsley, renowned Civil Rights attorney.

"Good morning, Mayor. Your secretary wasn't at her desk."

The Mayor looked passed him to confirm his words. She wasn't anywhere to be seen.

"What can I do for you, Mr. Billingsley?" After he heard the words, the Mayor realized he should have asked a different question.

"I believe you know why I'm here." Billingsley was still standing.

Walking around to his desk, the Mayor gestured for Billingsley to have a seat. Both men sat and stared at each other trying to feel the other out.

"Mayor, I believe I can help you with damage control." Billingsley wasted no time starting the conversation.

"Yeah? Just how do you propose to do that?" The Mayor was unconvinced.

"The answer is simple. Drop the Sundown rule, make a statement admitting the town has been wrong and add a sincere apology to it. With me standing by your side, I believe you can get ahead of this madness." Randolph Billingsley was responsible for ending peaceful demonstrations across the country.

"What makes you think I am not ahead of it?" The Mayor was not pleased with Billingsley trying to have the upper hand.

Billingsley chuckled. "If you were ahead of it Mayor, you wouldn't have a hundred news reporters spread all over this town and hundreds of protesters with more to surely come. If that's what you call being ahead of this, then no wonder Anna is in the situation it's in. Have you also considered the legal ramifications of this?

"What legal ramifications?" The Mayor was clueless in where Billingsley was going with this question.

"I suspect you will get a visit from the SBI. If what was shared in the interview about the arson was correct. If you are responsible for it in any way, you can expect a visit."

Sitting across from the Mayor was a man who knew his way around the law, and the Mayor knew Billingsley had the upper hand. The SBI wasn't on his radar and for a split second he thought again about Ridley. Normally, Ridley would be advising him in such matters. But not today, or any other day.

"What's in it for you?" The Mayor wanted to know.

"Nothing. Just justice for the people. You know the sooner you settle this, the less likely Anna will end up being sued for its discrimination. End it now Mayor and save the town from further humiliation. Think of it as my goodwill gesture for the decade. By the way, where is your legal counsel? Haven't you been advised on this? Oh, wait a minute. Your counsel is a victim. Well Mayor, you have a decision to make, and I suggest you make it soon. I'm not sure about the SBI, but if I had to guess, they will be here before too long. I strongly advise you to lawyer up. Just bringing things to your attention."

Billingsley didn't wait for the Mayor to answer, he just rose to his feet and walked out of the office. Trying to avoid the reporters, Billingsley slipped out the same way he came in, from the back of the building. This time the secretary was at her desk. Confused to see a black man come from the Mayor's office, she ran to see if the Mayor was okay.

With a light tap, she peeped her head through the door. "Are you alright, Mayor?"

Agitated that Billingsley was able to get to him in the first place, he was rigid with his response. "Where the hell have you been?" The Mayor didn't wait for her to answer. "You have to remain at your desk to prevent things like this from happening."

"I just went to the bathroom Mayor." The secretary sounding like a scolded child.

Feeling a bit embarrassed by his action, he apologized to her for his tone.

"I'm sorry I don't mean to be insensitive, but we are in a dire situation as you are fully aware. Since my guards are working overtime between helping outside with this madness and the hospital with Irene, I need you to be at your desk as much as possible. I do apologize for the way I came off." He was sorry for his behavior. The stress of everything was getting to him.

"Don't worry about it Mayor. I do understand. What's going to happen to our town?"

"I don't know. I just don't know." The Mayor shook his head.

No sooner than the words came from his mouth, the shattering of glass immediately got their attention. Within seconds the room filled with smoke, the Mayor grabbed his secretary by the hand and headed for an exit. Unsure of the device, they raced for the back door. They opened the door and headed for the Mayor's car. In their haste to leave, the Mayor didn't think about the reporters at the end of the road. Immediately they were bombarded with reporters blocking it. With cameras flashing, the Mayor was caught off guard. Trying not to injure anyone, he called for one of the officers to clear the road. He also told them about the device thrown through the window. The officer insisted to escort the Mayor home. The Mayor told him he wasn't going home and needed for him to stay there. He had a plan and would be safe. Within a few minutes the officers cleared the road for the Mayor to drive through. Once through the crowd, the Mayor called Brian, his head of security and told him what happened and where to meet him.

The Mayor's next instinct was to call Ridley. He had to get used to him not being a part of his life. It was hard though, they'd worked side by side for years.

The Mayor had a cousin who owned a diner out on route 273. He was headed there to meet with Brian. There was a place in the back of the diner where they would not be disturbed. Once the plans were in motion, the Mayor asked his secretary if she was okay. She nodded yes. No words were exchanged the rest of the drive. The only sound was the breathing between them. When they arrived at the diner, the Mayor pulled around the back and turned off the engine. Still neither one spoke. The guard tapped on the window lightly. He didn't want to startle the already rattled Mayor. The Mayor looked at Brian and made his way out of the car. His secretary followed. Exchanging mindless pleasantries, the three entered the diner through the back door. The Mayor's cousin was expecting them. Walking down the short hallway with the smell of grease meeting them with each step, they made haste toward the office. The cousin was in the office with glasses of iced tea. After offering them food which they declined, he left them to their business. The office was fairly clean and somewhat organized. The Mayor, his secretary and the body guard chose their seats and started planning a strategy.

Brian spoke first. "Is it true something was thrown through your window?"

"Hell yeah, it's true! You think I would make this up?" Agitation exuded from the Mayor.

Brian knew the Mayor was on edge, and his response just proved how much. Ignoring it, he continued with his questions. "When do we stop focusing on Irene and get back to the real job of protecting you?"

"I am not ready for her to be unattended just yet. Irene's caused enough chaos. So, until this goes away, I need for you and the team to make yourselves available to do both. Hopefully, this won't go on too much longer." The Mayor sounded calmer.

Brian knew better, but he indulged him in his thinking. The last few days had been tense for everyone. He couldn't begin to imagine how so for him. "Yes, Mayor. Whatever you need sir."

The three sat and talked for hours trying to figure out how something as simple as a dinner had turned into a fiasco. The Mayor hadn't told anyone about Ridley except for the guys sent to torch his place. His instructions were to make it look like an accident. The Mayor hadn't wanted to make that call but felt the pressure from the townsfolk to do something. When the town found out, they would never want to occupy the house anyway, so this would alleviate what he knew was coming. The Mayor agonized within himself over the things he'd done for the "preservation of Anna," as he'd been constantly reminded. He wasn't exactly sure when he compromised everything he believed and bought into the belief of the town. Maybe it was when his wife was struggling in her addiction. He may have allowed something he shouldn't have to take place. He wasn't sure. It started too many years back for him to recall.

The "accidental fire" would have worked though, had Ridley not anticipated his move. His partnering with Sharon Swanson to record it was brilliant on his part. No one else would have dared make such a move. He knew Ridley was a smart man and one hell of an attorney.

The anxiety return as he tried to silence the thoughts so loudly talking in his head. He could replay, recount and regret a lot of things but it wouldn't change his current situation.

The secretary nor Brian were equipped to help him, but they were sincerely trying to arrive at a workable solution to Anna's impending demise. The reality was Anna would have to make major changes. With the spotlight on them now, there wasn't any way of getting around it. Billingsley was correct in his expert assessment. They could possibly face criminal charges, but the Mayor wouldn't dare admit it to him. He also understood that standing with Billingsley to show a united front would never work, no matter how much he was willing to try it. The town folk wouldn't stand for it.

The three decided it was time to hold a press conference. The Mayor's secretary would draft a statement for him to address the media. The press conference would be scheduled for the day after tomorrow. Above all else, he was still the Mayor, and had a duty to the townspeople. He owed them an explanation and planned to address the residents of Anna first. It would be one of the hardest things he'd have to do in his career. Having tried to address this very issue years prior, the Mayor knew what he was about to face. There was old money in Anna and it talked. He wasn't convinced it was going to work this time though. Change had arrived in the form of Pearl Swanson and Benjamin Ridley. Anna just wasn't ready to embrace it yet.

The meeting was scheduled with the town folk the next day at noon, and it was for the residents of Anna only.

Chapter 31

The Town Meeting

The day of the meeting, the folk arrived in the same place where a couple of weeks ago they'd met to honor Pearl. Many were angry, while others came because of their insatiable appetite for gossip. The event hall was to capacity. After standing in line to show identification for entry many of the residents were appalled. This was the Mayor's attempt of keeping out the media and protesters. The time had come for a heart to heart talk with the residents. It was imperative for them to understand what to expect in the days and weeks to come. While waiting for the Mayor to take the stage, the residents talked among themselves in speculation. The consensus wanted to know where was Irene? It was obvious the Mayor had her in seclusion. These were smart, educated people, and they knew more was going on than the Mayor let on. Hopefully this meeting would bring them answers. Most of the residents were determined they would not leave the meeting until they got the answers they were looking for.

The Mayor suffered from sleep deprivation. The last thing he wanted was to face the people of Anna today. He was exhausted, unsure of many things, but with protesters and reporters parked in his town, he couldn't stall any longer. When the knock on the door came to let him know everyone had arrived, a lumped formed in his throat. It felt like he'd swallowed a golf ball. Putting on his suit jacket, he stood in front of the mirror, ran his fingers through his thinning hair, adjusted his tie, and sighed. Brian opened the door for them to head toward the stage.

Before taking the stage, the Mayor paused. Brian questioned his hesitation.

"I'm fine Brian," answered the Mayor.

Reaching for the rail to step to the stage, each step harder than the one before, he finally made it to the podium. The audience sat quietly and was very attentive.

"Good afternoon." The Mayor took a deep breath. He stood silent for a few seconds looking over the crowd. It was eerily quiet as each resident waited for answers.

"We have had one hell of a shock over the last couple of weeks. (Pause) I want to thank you for your patience as we tried to sort out the information we received regarding Pearl Swanson. We are now able to confirm what was shared by Irene Pritchard is true." (Pause)

The murmuring from the crowd started immediately. A man dressed in a starched white shirt and hard-pressed gray slacks, stood. His tone intentional. "How are you going to handle this Mayor?"

"Yeah!" The crowd responded in unison.

"Please allow me to get through my speech. I promise, I will answer your questions. You will hear things you will not like, but I must say them to you, to prepare you for what is to come."

The man still stood. Ready to interrupt again if things didn't go to his liking. He stared at the Mayor with a questioning look.

The Mayor ignoring the look, continued. *"Many of you will recall years ago when I attempted to address the Sundown rule…….."*

Immediately the man interrupted again. "What does that have to do with a black woman living in our town? I want to know what you are going to do about it Mayor? Stop dancing around the issue and give us answers."

"William, if you don't sit down and stop interrupting every time I try to say something, I will have you removed. This is your only warning." The Mayor's patience was wearing thin. He continued, cautiously.

"As you all are aware, we have become the spotlight for every news outlet as you can see, along with protesters because of the way we run things here in Anna. I don't know how we can go forward with

things as usual. Therefore, we are forced to make changes here in Anna."

The man once again opened his mouth to speak and was escorted out of the meeting. It didn't matter. More people began to show their dissatisfaction to the Mayor's speech. The Mayor rapped his gavel to restore order. It was crystal clear this meeting wasn't going as planned.

One of the officers blew his whistle in an attempt to quiet the hostile crowd. The same silent room the Mayor walked into a few minutes prior, returned.

"Folk, I assure you I am just as concerned as you are." In light of the media attention, we cannot proceed with our way of living. Besides, we've had two people living among us for years now. Has it really made a difference? Did they steal from you, harm you, diminish the value of Anna in any way?"

The Mayor raised his hand to stop any objections or interruptions.

"A couple of weeks ago, we all sat in this same place to honor Pearl for her fine years of service. Each one of us has benefitted some way or another by her being here. She has inspired us, served, and taught us things for many years. Many of you stood right here and applauded her for her contribution. Did those things mean nothing to us? We simply cannot continue to conduct ourselves in the manner that we have. Going forward, the Sundown Rule can no longer exist."

Anticipating the objections, he raised his hand again.

"Effective immediately, all people are welcome here in Anna. They are free to work and live here. They, of course, must afford the lifestyle, but discrimination will no longer exist."

"Have you lost your mind Mayor? Why would you think we would agree to this?" A man yelled from the front row. "This is our town. We control what goes on here. Always have, always will."

"Did you hear what I just said Robert? We don't have a choice in the matter. Not with the national attention. This is serious people. I have been informed to expect a visit from the SBI for criminal misconduct. I am not sure if that's valid, but it's a strong possibility."

Unable to keep control of the crowd because of the hurling questions, the Mayor allowed them to stand one at a time to express their concerns. If they became disruptive or threatening in any way, they would be removed.

"Where is Ridley? Was he behind this?" asked one man.

"Where is Irene?" asked a woman.

"This isn't about Ridley or Irene, the Mayor answered. This is about Anna. We don't have time to talk about either. You must agree to this change. Let's just do the right thing here and move on with our lives."

"I refuse to live among *those* people. I have lived here all of my life, and I don't want to start living with *them* now." An elderly woman in a black dress with white pearls responded.

"Well, Mrs. Thompson, I am afraid you may be looking for another place to live, if that's how you truly feel." The Mayor was growing weary in the direction of the meeting. "You all have the choice to leave if you don't want to conform to the new rule."

"Why should we leave our home," yelled a voice from the crowd.

The banter went on for almost an hour when finally, the Mayor took the last question and left the stage. The people stayed talking among themselves. Many were disappointed by the thought of having to live among *those people*. Others were down right outraged. Why would *they* even want to come? was the thought of most.

Back in the office of the event hall, the Mayor slumped in a chair. Physically tired and emotionally drained, he sat with his head in his hands.

"Can I get you anything Mayor?" Brian asked.

"No Brian. Unless you can make this nightmare go away, you can't get me anything. Just give me a minute. I will be ready to go home shortly."

Brian left the Mayor alone but stood outside the door.

The Mayor called his wife needing to hear a friendly voice.

"How did it go?" she asked after hearing his voice.

"It was as I expected…..brutal." Before the Mayor could finish his conversation with his wife, Brian knocked on the door, but didn't wait for a response. Opening the door, the Mayor was ready to reprimand him for the intrusion until he saw two men standing behind him wearing SBI jackets. He immediately told his wife he'd call her back. He knew everything Randolph Billingsley told him was starting to happen. This was the last thing he or the town needed right now.

Chapter 32

The Investigation

When the residents of Anna saw the arrival of the SBI, they realized the seriousness of what the Mayor had been trying to tell them. The SBI didn't waste any time delving into their investigation. Their main interests were the arson, who was behind it and the misconduct if any of the Mayor. The two investigators asked questions, looked at records and talked to residents of Anna and the people who worked for them. The help was reluctant to say anything in fear of losing their jobs. The investigators promised that wasn't going to happen, and they were there to make things better.

The Mayor now facing what he feared most, hired an attorney to represent him. How he wished it could have been Ridley. Even if things hadn't worked out the way it did, it would have been a conflict for him. The attorney he hired was nice enough and was astute in the law, so the Mayor felt he was being represented fairly. The harsh reality was the Mayor would probably face jail time for his role in the arson, if they had sufficient evidence to prove it. The men he hired to torch Ridley's house were on camera, so it would be hard to refute. His hope was they didn't find out about the other crimes that had taken place in the past. He felt terrible after each forced decision but told himself it was for "the good of Anna."

Each day was harder for the Mayor to face, not knowing when the investigation would be over. One of the hardest things he had to do was tell his wife the things he'd done to keep the people of Anna happy. He wasn't proud of them by any means, but she needed to know. The outcome of the investigation may not work out in his favor and he wanted her to be prepared. She was shocked. She wasn't oblivious to Anna's rule, but had no idea of the things her husband shared had taken place. The Mayor purposely kept her out of the affairs of his job. Besides, she had done well in her sobriety, and he hadn't wanted to jeopardize it in any way.

The days and weeks passed while the town waited for a decision regarding the investigation. Still, not wanting to accept abolishing the Sundown rule, the residents were adamant in standing their ground. It was rumored some were talking about leaving Anna before they would live among *those people*. Some had already spoken to real estate agents about selling. It was a serious situation for the residents. This quiet peaceful town was now flooded with change. Their privacy invaded by outsiders. Many blamed the Mayor for not knowing about Pearl or Ridley, since he'd worked so closely with both of them for years. The Mayor's argument was they also lived among them, and they didn't know it either. As much as they tried to live each day as normal as possible, there lay a dark cloud over Anna.

The reporters slowly left, but several remained waiting for the outcome of the investigation. Wanting to be the first to break the story, if there was one. The protesters came and went also, but things remained peaceful. They never found out who threw the smoke bomb in the Mayor's office. If someone knew, they weren't talking, at least not publicly.

One cloudy Thursday afternoon, the Mayor finally decided to go into the office. He'd been spending as much time with his wife, while they waited to hear from the SBI. His wife didn't want him to go. She told him about the nagging feeling she'd had all morning. He insisted on going if only for a little while. Not long after he arrived, had his morning coffee and looked through the stack of mail on his desk, his office door opened. It was the two investigators from the SBI. They did not bother to knock. When the Mayor looked up he knew this would be his last day as Mayor.

"Carter Henson, can you please stand?" one of the investigators asked rhetorically.

The Mayor stood reluctantly.

"Carter Henson, you are under arrest for hate crimes, abusing the power of your office, and blatant discrimination. You have the right to remain silent. Anything you say from this point will be used against you in a court of law. You have the right to an attorney. If you cannot afford one, one will be appointed to you. Do you understand the rights as I have read them to you?"

"Yes." The Mayor didn't say anything else.

The investigator cuffed the Mayor and led him out of the office. His secretary stood in disbelief with a tear streaming down her thin red cheek. She held one hand to her chest and the other to her mouth. Standing there not knowing what to say or do, she understood the seriousness of the matter.

"Call my attorney, and then call my wife," was the only thing the Mayor said to her as he was being escorted out the rear of the building. The cloudy day just grew darker.

Chapter 33

Pearl

"Good morning, my Queen." Andrew said to his mother as he entered the kitchen where Pearl was sitting.

"Good morning, my Prince." Pearl smiled as he kissed her forehead.

"You shouldn't be up. You still need your rest," Andrew showing concern for his mother.

"I've done nothing but rest these last few weeks, and I'm ready to get my life started again." Pearl let him know in no uncertain terms not to coddle her.

At that moment, Katelyn, David and Sharon joined them. Each poured a cup of coffee and sat with Pearl at the breakfast table. The prior weeks had been challenging as they worked to gain a sense of normalcy for their lives. They'd completed the tasks of unpacking and decorating to what they believed would be to their mother's satisfaction once she returned home. They'd finally gotten to the hospital to see her and after seeing where she was, they immediately wanted to move her. Dr. Parker and her staff had offered her excellent care, and Pearl made considerable improvement. When Ridley told them Dr. Parker was his daughter, who was a Board-Certified Neurologist, they felt more at ease with her course of treatment.

It wasn't long before Pearl regained movement first in her hand then her foot. The family was grateful the stroke hadn't caused any permanent damage. After working with a speech therapist, Pearl regained the ability to speak. Each day she grew stronger and stronger knowing her family hadn't abandoned her. She worked even harder to come home to them.

Remembering her visit from Ridley, it touched her deeply. He too had been afraid to share his secret, and like her, learned to bury it to have a decent life. She admired him and was thankful to him for confiding in her, but she often wondered how Irene had taken the news or if she even knew Ridley's secret.

Pearl sat at the round breakfast table looking at her children and their spouses. Her heart was full. Gratitude consumed her as she thought about their commitment to her. They'd put their lives on hold to be there. Even though her insistence for them to return home hadn't worked, part of her was glad they hadn't listened, they'd remained by her side. Pearl couldn't help but remember her husband and how proud he would be of the man and woman they'd become.

"What has you so deep in thought this morning mother?" Katelyn interrupted her mother's thoughts.

"Oh, nothing in particular, just a lot of random thoughts." Pearl took a sip of coffee and stared at each of them with her contagious smile.

"Pearl, I must say you are as beautiful as ever." David, who helped in her recovery when she returned home, said to her in a reassuring voice. They all agreed if someone saw her, who didn't know about the fiasco Irene caused, would not be able to tell she'd had a stroke.

Pearl's life was slowly returning to normal. Each day she gained strength. Although her family limited her activities, Dr. Parker had given her a clean bill of health. When Pearl was discharged from the hospital she was excited to get home. Katelyn and Andrew told her how they arranged for everything to be at the new house. Pearl was surprised at how much they'd managed to get done.

"Thank you David. You've been a very big help toward me, and I'm grateful to you," Pearl sounded a bit emotional addressing him. "Your patience has meant the world to me."

David raised his coffee cup to her.

"Now, I want you all to tell me what has happened since I've been away. You have kept things from me long enough." Pearl was insistent in wanting to know. The hospital wouldn't give her any information, so she had been completely in the dark on matters from the outside world. All she knew was she was in a hospital outside of Anna and Ridley had visited her and shared his secret. David had been in and out speaking with Dr. Parker and overseeing her care.

Katelyn was the first to speak. "Mother…"

Before she could get the rest of her words out, Pearl stopped her. "I don't want to hear it Katelyn. It has been long enough. You cannot protect me forever. I don't want to be treated or handled like one of the grandchildren, you've done that for far too long." The cup Pearl had been holding was now on the table.

"You're right mother," Andrew chiming in the conversation. "You deserve to know the truth, the entire truth.

In their own way, they each explained the events of Anna from the time she'd been taken to the hospital, the burning of Ridley's house, Irene slitting her wrist, the protesting, and the Mayor being arrested, including very vivid details.

Pearl sat quietly. It was a lot of information to take in. She wasn't sure how to process it all. If nothing else, it brought more questions than answers. It was hard for her to believe all these things had taken place in this peaceful town. Had all her efforts been in vain? Was she the reason Anna was turning? What about Irene?

Before long the grandchildren bounced down the stairs in their teenage fashion. Each greeting Pearl in their own way. The overwhelming love filled her heart. She loved her family. It was everything to her. Even in her moments of doubting, they more than proved their love toward her. She wasn't alone or abandoned after all.

The relief of her secret brought a new-found freedom for Pearl, especially since she was no longer in Anna. This was her new start. She loved her new home. For now, she would enjoy her family knowing they would leave soon. They certainly could not continue to put their lives and careers on hold. Pearl also knew the children would start school soon and needed to get back. Still, she enjoyed every second with them. She was especially grateful to Sharon. She handled the story of Anna in her usual professional manner. Pearl was sure Sharon would win an award for her outstanding journalism. When breakfast was over Pearl and Sharon sat out on the patio by the waterfall.

"I haven't had the opportunity to thank you," Pearl started the conversation.

Sharon was a bit unsure what the gratitude was for. "Thank me for…?"

"Being bold enough to tell the story of Anna. Many people knew the town's history but chose to turn the other way. But you…you had the courage to jump in and make the world aware of the injustice there."

"I am glad Ridley asked me to help. At the time, I wasn't sure of the magnitude of it all. I thought it was going to be another story until we went to his house that day. I was able to see firsthand, the length they were willing to go to keep the history of Anna preserved."

Pearl smirked at Sharon's choice of words. "You certainly know how to be *politically correct.*"

"May I ask you a question?" Sharon asked cautiously.

"You may ask me anything." By now you should know there are no more secrets," Pearl assured her.

"Once you knew Anna's secret, why did you stay?"

The two women sat on the wooden and wrought iron bench facing the cascading water, falling over the metal backdrop. It was a minute before Pearl spoke.

"The short answer is I'm not sure. When I first came to Anna, I was young and naïve. I also was escaping an ugly past. My parents felt it best if I left the south and came north for a better life. I didn't want to disappoint them. When I arrived, I found a room at the old boarding house, kept to myself, read and learned all I could to educate myself. I never passed up an opportunity to learn or try anything new. I modeled myself after the women I saw in Anna. They were well dressed, carried themselves in a way I'd never seen before. Little did they know I was a country girl, striving for better. I never intended to hide my ethnicity. The longer I stayed, the more I started to hear little things here and there. By that time, I was making decent money, started to fit in with people, and I liked the independence it brought. I was here about a year by the time I fully understood Anna. I met my husband soon after that and learned to keep my mouth shut," she paused.

Sharon wasn't sure if she stirred bad memories for Pearl or what. So, she sat waiting for Pearl to make the next move. She looked around at the breath-taking beauty the yard held. It was like a sanctuary. The landscaping company Andrew hired, did a fantastic job sculpting out flower beds and seating areas, with edging along the walkway. Not to mention, perfectly placed yard statues. It wasn't too much, it looked like a page from a magazine. Sharon closed her eyes, breathing in the fresh air, still waiting for Pearl to continue.

"There were times Doc and I talked about leaving Anna," Pearl resumed the conversation. "We would talk at night after Andrew and Katelyn were asleep. We didn't want them to grow up in such a narrow-minded town. How we wanted them to have exposure and experiences beyond Anna, but Doc loved his work. It was hard to walk away from it, so we stayed....I stayed."

Pearl looked at Sharon with a sadness in her face. Almost as if it was regret. Sharon wasn't sure. She couldn't imagine having to be in such a situation. Intrigued by the details of Pearl's life, she wanted to hear more, but didn't want to push her. It wouldn't be fair. Sharon knew Pearl was sharing information with her that Andrew and Katelyn didn't know. She was sure of it. Just as she'd promised Katelyn not to share her secrets, Sharon felt the same about Pearl's.

"I'm sorry you had to hide something so important in order to have a better life." Sharon was empathetic in her remark. "Look at what you've accomplished despite the fact of a backwards town. You've raised two amazing human beings. I know them both, so I know that wasn't easy." She laughed trying to bring laughter to such a heavy conversation.

Pearl laughed in agreement with Sharon. "We had our moments for sure."

Andrew came out to join the ladies, infringing on their conversation.

"What are you too so engrossed in?" he asked.

The women looked at each other letting out hearty laughter.

"Wouldn't you like to know?" Sharon winked at Pearl.

"Some things are better kept between us women," Pearl winked back at Sharon. The two women continued in their laughter.

Pearl kissed Andrew on the cheek. "You know I love you son." She rose and walked into the house leaving Sharon and Andrew alone.

"What was that about?" asking his wife.

"Wouldn't you like to know?" Sharon kissed the other cheek, slid her arm in his and laid her head on Andrew's shoulder.

Chapter 34

A New Friend

After lunch Pearl took a short nap. Keeping in line with the Dr.'s orders, she wanted to continue with her progress. Although she felt great, she remained obedient. Later in the day Pearl had an unexpected visitor. She was in the kitchen making a pitcher of lemonade when the doorbell rang. Andrew answered the door.

"Ridley. It's good to see you." Andrew embraced him as he entered the foyer.

Ridley moved with his daughter, when he'd learned Pearl was coming home. He wanted to give her enough time to get settled into her normal routine before visiting. He felt today would be the perfect day.

When Pearl heard Ridley's voice, she washed her hands and went out to greet him. They each stood staring at one another before they hugged. Just like the unspoken rule in Anna had been carried on for years, Pearl felt they now had an unspoken special bond between them.

"Come in and make yourself at home," Pearl insisted. "I was making lemonade, would you like a glass?"

"Only if it's no trouble," replied Ridley.

"Why don't you both sit, and I will bring the lemonade." Andrew was out of the room before Pearl could object.

"You look well." Ridley started the conversation. "My daughter seems pleased with your progress."

"Thank you. Your daughter is an extraordinary doctor. I don't think I would be where I am if it wasn't for her. You should be very proud."

"I am. She has done well for herself. My only regret is she settled for a smaller hospital when she could have been doing greater things elsewhere."

"Yes. But had she been elsewhere I may not have gotten the treatment I received."

"You are correct. I told you how well you looked, but how are you feeling?" Ridley asked out of concern.

"I feel almost as good as I did before the stroke." Pearl was being honest. She really felt close to her normal self.

Andrew finally returned with lemonade, cheese, crackers and grapes. Pearl was never disappointed with him. He went the extra mile in everything he did.

"How are you?" Pearl asked Ridley as she took the glass of lemonade Andrew offered her.

"Adjusting." He took a sip of lemonade after his response. "I am sure you've been brought up to speed on the events over the last few weeks."

"Yes, I think I am up to speed."

"I want to apologize to you Pearl," he paused.

"Apologize for what? You have nothing to apologize for." Pearl looked confused.

"The night I came to your hospital room. I never meant to dump my story on you that way. I was so upset from what Irene had done and what happened to you. I genuinely came out of concern for your well-being knowing Katelyn and Andrew needed to protect your grandchildren from the ugliness that had just taken place. I never meant to upset you in any way." Ridley sipped his lemonade and continued. "In some way I wanted you to know you were not alone. I failed obviously in my attempt to…"

"Stop. It meant the world to me. I must admit I was confused and a bit agitated with you rambling on, but when I thought about it all, I was appreciative of you confiding in me. I know how it feels to carry something for years, unable to share it with anyone. So, don't sit there and think you owe me an apology because you don't."

Andrew looked at his mother and then at Ridley. In his time with Ridley over the past few weeks, he'd grown to respect him more and more for who he was and what he did. Just like his mother, all Ridley wanted was a better way of life. They just happened to land in Anna to get it. But now, in the presence of two people Andrew admired the most, he felt privileged to know them beyond the obvious relationships. They didn't make them like this anymore.

"Thank you Pearl. You are an amazing woman. I am glad to get to know you beyond Ir...," Ridley stopped before finishing her name.

"You can say her name. Irene was a large part of both our lives for years. We can't erase it, nor would I want to. We both knew how she could be. We just didn't think she would turn on us. I think we both wanted to see the good in her."

Ridley felt a sense of relief. Just like that night in the hospital, he didn't come to upset Pearl, only to see how she was.

"May I ask you, Ridley, what drew Irene to slitting her wrist? I didn't get those details. Apparently, no one knew."

"I told her the truth," said Ridley. "Irene couldn't handle it. She tried to take the cowards way out."

"Why would you tell her now?" Pearl couldn't understand the timing.

"Oh, she didn't tell you? We were going to be married. Irene wanted to wait until after your celebration to announce it. Now I understand why she wanted to wait. When I tried to talk to her after it was over, she was still her smug, arrogant, privileged self. I couldn't reason with her. She felt no remorse for what she'd done to you. The only way I knew to make her feel some inkling of what she'd done, was to tell her the truth. Of course, Irene didn't believe me. Told me I was being cruel. I assured her I wasn't, and then I left. I found out later about the suicide attempt."

"My goodness!" Pearl exclaimed. "Marriage? Irene Pritchard agreed to marry you?" She couldn't believe it.

"Yes. Irene agreed, reluctantly, but she did. It wasn't until I threatened to walk away from the relationship that she did. You know Irene, everything has to be on her terms but not with this."

"The one thing I never thought she would do." Pearl sat shaking her head. "Where is she now? Do you know? Have you seen her, or talked with her?"

"No. I have no desire to do either. I loved her once. I'm sure a part of me always will, but not enough to have any kind of relationship with her. I am certain she doesn't want to see me either."

Pearl sat across from Ridley looking at this man neatly dressed in brown slacks and a starched beige shirt. His winged tip shoes were freshly buffed and showed no signs of dust or debris. He fidgeted with the signet ring on his pinkie finger as he crossed his long legs. Pearl always thought he was a handsome man, but now as she stared at him he looked very distinguished. There was a distinct air about him. She could see why Irene wanted him to herself. In getting to know more about Ridley, Pearl could see Irene may have thought she controlled him, but Pearl was beginning to see who really controlled their relationship.

As they continued in conversation, the phone rang. Katelyn interrupted and handed the phone to her mother. Pearl excused herself to take the call. Surprised to learn it was the Governor on the other end.

Pearl had met the Governor on a few occasions when he attended a ball or made an appearance for special town dinners or fund raisers. She could not imagine why he was calling her.

"Pearl, I am aware of the trouble in Anna." The Governor wasted no time speaking when Pearl answered the phone. "I plan to be there at the end of the week. I would like to meet with you while I'm there if your schedule permits."

"Governor, I am not sure what this is about. I am still recovering from my stroke; my family is here, and I no longer live in Anna."

"I am aware of all of that Pearl, and I wouldn't ask if it wasn't important. If it makes it any easier, I can come to you." The Governor wasn't taking no for an answer.

"I would feel better if you came here, if you must. Can you tell me what this is about?" Pearl was curious about the meeting."

"I will explain everything to you on Friday. I should be there by noon."

Before Pearl could get another word out, he was gone. Walking back into the den with the others, they could see a look of concern on her face.

"Is everything alright Mother?" Katelyn asked.

"I'm not sure." Pearl made her way back to the sofa.

"It was the Governor wanting to meet with me on Friday of this week."

"What on earth for?" Katelyn sounding agitated wanted to know.

"He wouldn't say. Just said we would talk about it on Friday."

Pearl seemed a bit confused by it all. There was nothing she could do until she heard what he had to say on Friday.

"Would you like for me to be here in case there are legal matters he may want to discuss? Ridley was quick to offer his services to her.

"I would like that very much." Pearl thanked Ridley for the offer.

Sharon, David and Jon had started dinner. Pearl tried to get Ridley to stay, but he didn't want to intrude. He left, said he wanted to take his daughter to dinner, but would see them on Friday.

Chapter 35

The Governor

Friday morning the entire house rose early to prepare for the Governor. Pearl was feeling better and back to her normal routine of fussing over everyone. She baked a variety of pastries, cooked a hearty breakfast and started lunch for the Governor. She wasn't sure if it was necessary, but it calmed her nerves as she anticipated what he wanted from her.

Sharon and Katelyn offered their assistance several times throughout the morning, but Pearl rejected it wanting to have time to herself to think. She'd given them instructions on dusting and making the house presentable. David and Andrew suggested they all leave to give Pearl time with the Governor. Katelyn and Sharon refused. They wanted to be present when the Governor arrived. After David and Andrew lost the battle they decided to take the children out later. Besides they wanted to stay also to hear what the Governor had to say. David put Jon in charge of the other children while the adults waited. They wouldn't have to wait long.

At 11:59, the doorbell rang. The Governor's bodyguard stood at the door, tall, well dressed and very stoic. Without hesitation, the guard introduced himself and requested to sweep the premises. Not waiting for a response, he walked passed Pearl to start his "sweep." The women looked at each other in questionable disbelief. He'd gone through the entire house within a matter of minutes. Without saying a word, he motioned for the other guard to escort the Governor out of the car. The Governor walked toward the house where Pearl and the other four were waiting. He entered and shook Pearl's hand. Pearl introduced him to the other four, then she invited him to have a seat. She informed him Ridley would be joining them shortly. Within a few minutes, the doorbell rang again and true to his word, Ridley made his way past the guard and joined the group inside. After pleasantries, the Governor began the conversation.

"Pearl, I am glad to see you are recovered from your illness. As you know, Anna is in dire straits right now. I am pretty sure the Mayor is going to prison and is prepared to resign. Because Anna is too small to have a formal council, I must put an interim Mayor in place, until we can hold a special election."

No one expected this. They could not understand why the Governor was having this conversation with Pearl. Not even Pearl understood where he was going.

"Just bear with me for a minute and hear me out. Anna is in a delicate position right now. The changes I want to see here requires someone of…"

"STOP RIGHT THERE, GOVERNOR!" Katelyn didn't want to hear anymore he had to say. He surely wasn't about to ask her mother what she thought he was going to ask her. It wasn't possible.

All eyes were on Katelyn as her behavior startled everyone, but in unison they all turned their attention right back to the Governor. He waited for a few seconds and resumed.

"The changes can only occur if someone who already knows the people, can lead Anna into the future. You are the only person I know capable of handling the job." The Governor sat on the edge of his seat as he made his pitch to Pearl.

No one spoke. They probably were thinking the same thing Katelyn voiced, but were too shocked to voice it. Where had the Governor been the last few weeks? How could he ask such nonsense to a woman who could have lost her life over the backward thinking of this town. He couldn't be serious.

Pearl sat in silence. Looking at the face of Andrew, Katelyn, Sharon, David and finally Ridley, she was uncertain to what she'd heard. Each looked back at her questionably. Pearl purposefully did not look at the Governor. Her heart was pounding. Her head swirling with words that refused to form sentences.

"I know this is a lot to ask," the Governor spoke as if he was reading everyone's thoughts. "But if Anna is going to move forward, its only chance is to have someone who loves the town, the people, and is capable of strong leadership. Yes, there will be heavy resistance, some will even leave Anna. That's a good thing. We want the ones to leave who will not be willing to embrace the change."

Still, everyone remained silent. When the Governor realized he wasn't about to get a response from Pearl in that moment, he stood with both hands folded in front of him.

"Take some time to think about it. Again, I know this comes as a total shock to you. It's also a big decision. Talk it over with your family and get legal advice if you feel it's necessary. I will call you in a few days."

Still standing as if waiting for someone to escort him out, the Governor headed toward the door. He turned one last time to look at the cluster of people who were unmoved before leaving.

The six adults remained quiet for a long time. No one knew what to say, so they leaned forward, backward, repositioned and paused, but spoke not one word. Katelyn eventually broke the silence. She was never one to back down from any confrontation.

"The nerve of that man, I don't care if he is the Governor! Surely he couldn't think you would consider such utter foolishness!" She was up walking around.

"I think it makes perfect sense." Ridley spoke in a soft tone but never looked up. All eyes were focused on him.

"Mother, what are your thoughts?" Andrew asked Pearl, ignoring Ridley's comment.

"I simply don't know what to think. I can't comprehend any of it right now."

"She is getting over a stroke. She can't possibly consider this. Besides, it's ludicrous." Katelyn wasn't willing to entertain the thought in any way.

"Think about it. I believe the Governor is correct. Pearl has been a major influence in Anna. If anyone can turn Anna around, it would be her. But only if she is willing to take on the challenge and it would be a challenge," Ridley spoke confidently now.

"Don't speak about me as if I am not here in the room," Pearl quickly chimed in. "This is overwhelming for me right now, so I'm not able to make a comment one way or the other. It is farfetched, but I would like to take some time to consider what has been offered."

"Moth….." Katelyn started to speak but Pearl cut her off.

"Save your breath Katelyn. I'm not going to talk about this now. I'm going to my room and lie down. You all can discuss it all you want but without me."

On that note, Pearl left the room and went down the hall to her bedroom. Once inside she sat on the side of her bed and cried. The same spot where she cried before her celebration dinner and now for such an opportunity offered to her by the Governor. It was entirely too much to process. Pearl didn't know what to think or how to feel. Normally, this was when she would call Irene. The thought made her cry even harder. She didn't know whether to curse Irene or thank her. None of this would be a possibility if she hadn't exposed Pearl's secret. So many thoughts. So many decisions. It was too much. She went to the bathroom washed her face, crawled onto her bed and fell into a deep sleep.

Postlude

Three months after the Governor's visit, the interim Mayor took office. Things in Anna certainly were changing. Just as they all suspected, people who had ruled the town for years left without hesitation. Others remained, resistant in the beginning, but overtime, the dark cloud was lifting from Anna.

The integration was beginning, and new families were being welcomed into Anna without incident. The town was broadcasting on radio stations, tv stations and print advertisements that all people were welcome in the town. It wasn't long before the remaining residents felt comfortable getting to know the newcomers. Change didn't come over night, but all were confident they were on the right path.

Businesses were growing, and people of color were bringing business to Anna. The town was flourishing even more.

The protesting eventually died down. The weeks the protesters were in Anna were peaceful. Everyone wanted the same thing in the end. Equality.

The former mayor took a plea deal and was sentenced to 5 years in federal prison with 3-years suspended. His wife stood by him during the trial and chose to remain in Anna. The judge considered his attempts to overcome the injustice but told him he could have stepped away at any time and not participated in the "Sundown Rule." The judge granted some leniency but couldn't allow him to go unpunished. The mayor took the blame and refused to name names. The men caught on video by Sharon pled guilty and each received a year in prison for arson.

Irene never recovered mentally from the attempt on her life. Every time she thought about her years with Ridley, she fell back into a deep depression. She lived her remaining days in a psychiatric facility. Irene would never see the new Mayor take office.

The day the Mayor addressed the town of Anna after the swearing in ceremony, the town hall was full. Reporters flooded the room. This was a historical event. It was standing room only. The Mayor was surprised and overcome with joy. Life had come full circle for a woman who only wanted a chance at a decent life. As Pearl took the stage with her deputy mayor Ridley beside her, the people stood and applauded. Her family was there in full support. Even though Katelyn fought the decision every step of the way, she was proud of her mother. This was a new day for everyone. By taking the stage Pearl was burying the separation of the old "Anna" and the stigma attached to it. It would be the last time the phrase, **"Ain't No Negros Allowed"** (ANNA) would be used.

Look for "Anna"

The sequel to Pearl

Spring 2019

Find out what happens in the aftermath. Will Pearl remain Mayor? What happens to Irene? Will peace continue in Anna?

About the Author

Debra Funderburk is the ultimate Serial-Prenuer. Whether coaching writers through The Charlotte Writing Academy, educating them by way of The Charlotte Write to Publish; a monthly writers' group, or publishing aspiring authors through Burkwood Media; her days are filled with writing, marketing or publishing. When she manages to find free time, it is spent with her husband of thirty-five years, her children and grandchildren.

Feel free to contact Debra for information regarding writing, publishing, business coaching for authors, workshops or speaking engagements.

www.debrafunderburk.com

debrawfunderburk@gmail.com

www.ingramcontent.com/pod-product-compliance
Lightning Source LLC
Chambersburg PA
CBHW061922130726
47908CB00016B/969